Tell Everyone I Said Hi

The

John

Simmons

Short

Fiction

Award

University of

Iowa Press

Iowa City

Chad Simpson

Tell Everyone I Said Hi

Fic
Sim

University of Iowa Press, Iowa City 52242

Copyright © 2012 by Chad Simpson

www.uiowapress.org

Printed in the United States of America

The University of Iowa Press is a member of Green Press
Initiative and is committed to preserving natural resources.
Printed on acid-free paper

Library of Congress Cataloging-in-Publication Data

Simpson, Chad.

Tell everyone I said hi / by Chad Simpson.

     p. cm.—(The John Simmons short fiction award)

ISBN-13: 978-1-60938-126-4, ISBN-10: 1-60938-126-2 (pbk)

ISBN-13: 978-1-60938-141-7, ISBN-10: 1-60938-141-6 (ebook)

I. Title.

PS3619.I56327T45 2012

813'.6—dc23   2012007869

For my wife, Jane,

and

in memory of my mom

Contents

ACKNOWLEDGMENTS

These stories first appeared in the following publications: "Miracle," *SmokeLong Quarterly*; "Fostering" (as "Especially Roosevelt"), *The Sun*; "The Woodlands," *American Short Fiction*; "Peloma," *McSweeney's Quarterly*; "Let x," *Esquire*; "fourteen," *matchbook*; "Obnubilate," *The Collagist*; "Tell Everyone I Said Hi," *Avery: An Anthology of New Fiction*; "Glass," *Guernica*; "American Bulldog," *Crab Orchard Review*; "Adaptations," *Necessary Fiction*; "House Calls," *Hobart*; "The First Night Game at Wrigley," *New South*; "Potential," BULL: *Men's Fiction*; "Estate Sales," *juked*; "Two Weeks and One Day," *Keyhole Digest*.

"Fostering" (as "Especially Roosevelt") was reprinted in *You Must Be This Tall to Ride: Contemporary Writers Take You Inside the Story*. "American Bulldog" was reprinted in *New Stories from the Midwest 2011*. "Miracle," "The Woodlands," "Let x," "Glass," "House Calls," "Estate Sales," and "Two Weeks and One Day" were published as part of *Phantoms*, a chapbook released by Origami Zoo Press.

Thanks to Craig Watson, Agi Zivaljevic, Beth Lordan, Brady Udall, Rodney Jones, Jon Tribble, Allison Joseph, Jane Cogie, Donna Strickland, Benjamin Percy, Justin Hamm, Clint Cargile, Keith Russell, Matt Garrison, Ethan Castelo, Robin Metz, Monica Berlin, Lori Haslem, Rob Smith, Emily Anderson, Sean Mills, Bob and Virginia Hellenga, Cyn Kitchen, Anne Giffey and Rob Budach, Eugene Cross, Amy Greene, Matt Debenham, Nat Akin, Marsha McSpadden, Amanda Lisle, Steve Davenport, Okla Elliott, Katrina Denza, Randall Brown, Eli Horowitz, B. J. Hollars, Jason Lee Brown, Marian Oman, Steve Himmer, Jamie Iredell, Jarrett Haley, Kathy Fish, John Wang, Claudia Smith, Kyle Minor, Ethel Rohan, Brian Mihok, Edward Mullany, Matt Bell, Scott Garson, Jensen Beach, Rebecca King, Aaron Burch, Stephanie Fiorelli, Adam Koehler, Peter Cole, Meakin Armstrong, Jenn De Leon, Laura van den Berg, Kiki Petrosino, Cathy Chung, Justin Torres, Southern Illinois University Carbondale, Knox College, the Illinois Arts Council, the Bread Loaf Writers' Conference, and the Sewanee Writers' Conference.

To all of my students: You've helped keep me in this game. You've taught me so much.

To Jane, Dad, Brent and Becky, Grandma Carolyn, Aunt Sharon, Rob Bob and Vic, Jil and Scott, Joy, and the rest of my family and friends: I am forever grateful for your patience and kindness, your generosity and love and grace.

*Tell
Everyone
I Said
Hi*

Miracle

My brother calls and says to get to the bar as fast as I can—he thinks he just died.

Later, he will show me the bruise—a tire-wide swath of mottled purple and pale green—streaked up the inside of his thigh and the middle of his chest, where his own car ran him over. He will be high on something, and half-feral, and he will call it a miracle: how the tire track stops just below his neck; how the car didn't crush him.

And I will imagine him standing next to his car as it began to roll downhill. I will imagine him catching up to the car and getting behind it, putting up his hands like he's Superman stopping a train. I will imagine the car running straight over him.

I will laugh because that's what I'm conditioned to do. I won't tell him how many times I have woken in the middle of the night—my heart beating like a wild thing in my chest—having dreamed him dead.

When I pull up to the stoplight across from the bar, my brother is lying on his back where it happened, and his friends are making an outline of his body on the street with masking tape. Before I decide to just keep going, I watch him lie there, perfectly still, his hands splayed at his sides. His friends try to work the tape around one of my brother's boots, but the tape keeps getting twisted, folding over on and sticking to itself. His friends laugh, ecstatic, and tear at the tape with their teeth.

I wish I could join them. Instead, I train my eyes on my brother's chest.

He still thinks he may be dead, and his heart. Beneath his shirt, where the bruise has not yet begun to form, his heart is racing. His breath, I can tell from where I'm sitting, it can hardly keep up.

You
Would've
Counted
Yourself
Lucky

The boy's sister is missing or has not yet come home. It's only 9:30, still too early to tell, but she was supposed to have the car in the garage and her own two feet on their property by seven.

The boy's mom says to his dad, "Did you get the yard mowed before it got dark?"

The boy's dad answers, "Is that your third Beam and Coke or your fourth?"

What they are really saying to one another, the boy knows, is, *I hope Leanne isn't still over at Ledarius's house.*

Only the boy thinks his sister might be missing. He kind of hopes she is. He kind of hopes that what's going on here isn't the same old same old, that there's something more mysterious and tragic stirring just beneath the surface of these latest events, about to erupt like hot lava from an old volcano.

But the truth is his parents don't like the fact that Leanne keeps dating black guys. All summer long, ever since she got her driver's license in June and began dating Tony, the first of three black boys, all younger than her, she's been saying to her parents, "It's 2010. Think about who's in the White House." Her parents have been saying back, "That doesn't make it right."

The boy listens from his bedroom to his parents yelling more questions at one another and plays a video game on his handheld. The screen is cracked. The emitted music is damaged, warped—the notes last longer than they should and are slightly off-key. After a while, he tosses it onto his bed and starts sketching a dinosaur in his drawing book.

He is ten, too old to draw dinosaurs according to most of the kids in his class at school, but it's not like he's just tracing them out of some stained book from the library. He is creating them.

This one has a head much too small for his body, super-short arms and tiny hands with enormous thumbs. This one has tattoos on his belly and lips that are caved in like the lips on old people or meth-heads. He likes the way this looks. When he puts the finishing touches on it—a half moon of bruise beneath one of the dinosaur's eyes and a pair of broken glasses ringed with tape at the bridge—he laughs and closes the book.

In the living room, the boy's mom holds her drink in the air and says in this defeated way to the boy's dad, "Could you maybe just add a couple ice cubes to this?"

The boy's dad rises from his chair and says, "Sure." When he returns with the freshened drink he tells the boy's mom that he'll mow the yard first thing tomorrow.

It is just past ten o'clock. What they are really saying to one another is, *Do you have any idea how to proceed from here? When Leanne comes back, what are we going to say to her? What are we going to do?*

Neither one of them acknowledges the boy as he passes through the room. He feels, as is often the case, a little like a ghost. Just before he enters the kitchen, he raises his hands in the air and whispers, "Bwah-ha-ha-ha-ha."

He grabs a flashlight from under the sink and steps out the door that leads to the backyard. The door slams shut hard. It echoes in the thick and humid air, and the boy can feel the sound the door makes in the small of his back.

Near the garage, near the place where his sister should have parked the car over three hours ago—because tonight, just one night this week, her parents didn't want her driving god-knows-where at all hours of the night with that fifteen-year-old boy in the front seat with her—there is a basketball hoop and a large square of dirt in the yard where the boy has dribbled the grass dead. He clicks on his flashlight and crouches low, begins searching the dirt for earthworms.

It is mid-August, and the dirt is hard-packed and cracked like dry skin in the flashlight's beam. There is not an earthworm in sight. The boy wonders whether the worms are still living there in the ground. He wonders how deep they've had to burrow in order to find mud moist enough to move through.

He hovers his hand over the dirt and makes shapes in the air that cast cool-looking shadows onto the ground. Here is a bunny rabbit with fangs like samurai swords. Here is the meanest junk-yard dog in all of Kentucky. The boy is trying to remember what other things he knows how to make out of shadows when he hears a noise. He can't tell whether the maker of the sound is human or animal, but he is aware suddenly of the downy hairs, now gone stiff, on the back of his neck.

He clicks off the flashlight and sets it near his foot. The darkness for a moment transforms into its own living and breathing thing, and it occurs to him that he's gone earthworming in this same dark about a million times but never quite so late at night.

The boy listens for the sound, prepared to sprint toward his house's back door if necessary, but hears only the pulse of bugs, like the nighttime's beating heart. He picks up his flashlight and turns it back on.

First, he points the flashlight at the sky, which is starry and brilliant. He takes aim at a particularly bright star that might actually be a planet, high in the sky, and clicks the flashlight on and then off again a few times. The boy doesn't know Morse code, but he's pretty sure aliens don't either. He wonders how long it will take his little stutter of light to reach the stars. He wonders who will be there to translate what he has communicated when it does.

This is an easy and comforting line of thought for the boy. He loves the night sky over Kentucky. He loves the idea of aliens, of beings out there in the universe more powerful than anything here on earth. Beings capable of ending our little marble of a planet just because they were bored, in only seconds.

The boy is imagining a quickly destroyed world—water rising up out of the oceans, insects and birds falling from the sky, each and every human being's skin bubbling like milk in a pan on the stove and then turning to paste and dripping from their bones—when he hears the sound again. It's human, he realizes this time. It's a voice. It has just said, "You."

The boy clicks off his flashlight so that he can slip back into his backyard's darkness, in case the voice means to cause him harm.

"That didn't make you invisible, you know," the voice says. It is female. Older than him, he thinks, but not so old as his parents. Maybe his sister's age.

The boy turns the flashlight back on and swings it in a slow arc at the houses across the alley from him. Here is the Johnsons' busted trampoline. Here are their stacks of PVC pipe that've been sitting around forever, doing nothing but squashing grass. Next door, where an old lady who has her groceries delivered to her lives, there's a sad-looking doghouse with three holes in its roof and no pet in sight. The boy pauses the flashlight for a moment. He's not sure how it's possible, but it seems as though everything looks worse in his flashlight's beam than it does in the light of day. Everything seems to look more miserable and ruined. It's like the flashlight is revealing the place's true nature, which up until right then had been hidden from him in plain sight.

The boy can't believe that this is where he lives. That this is where he has been growing up. It's no wonder his sister has become the kind of person she has become.

"You're getting warmer," the voice says. "Keep going. Just one more house to your right."

It's kind of an ugly voice, the boy realizes. It sounds like it is coming from a girl who is chewing the insides of her cheeks while she talks, and he recognizes it now. He hasn't heard it for months, not since school let out, but it's Rebecca.

Heat lightning flashes in the sky over the row of houses across the alley, and the boy imagines for a second that someone out in space is responding to the blips of light he'd sent up that way a little bit ago. Whoever it is, the boy thinks, they have misinterpreted his signal. He'd meant it to be friendly.

The boy shines the flashlight in the direction of the next house over, and there is Rebecca. She is sitting on a screened-in back porch, and the boy can see most of her torso. The steel braces she uses to help her walk glint in the light. Rebecca shields her eyes. She says, "Down, boy. Holster your weapon."

The boy isn't sure what to do. He knows he should be nice to Rebecca—she's been through some sorrowful and agonizing shit—but she is mostly a total pain in the ass. He turns off the flashlight slowly and soundlessly and lets his arm fall to his side. He is still facing Rebecca's back porch, but if he began walking backward, he would reach his own house's back door in probably thirty steps. He would become invisible inside his own house again, and Rebecca would probably forget that she ever even saw him out there looking for earthworms, shining his flashlight at the sky, hoping his sister would just come home already. Hoping maybe she wouldn't.

Above him, the boy knows, there are stars that have been shining since fish had feet, and this, too, offers a kind of comfort. He wipes some sweat from his forehead and runs his hand through his hair, begins walking forward.

The story people tell about Rebecca goes like this: Two years ago she was as beautiful as any girl in Nelson County. She was a gymnast and a cheerleader. She liked history and had a decent GPA and dated a boy who was runner-up at the state wrestling meet in the 185-pound division. Then she went to a party one night in the summer before her senior year and got wasted on wine cooler–spiked gin. A little while later, she was in the passenger seat while some other gymnast/cheerleader-type was drunkenly navigating the bendy roads out near Maker's Mark.

The girl driving the car walked away from the wreck with a broken occipital bone and some superficial scratches. Rebecca shot through the windshield and past the tree the girl's car had collided with, the boy has heard told, like the prettiest cannonball ever.

Leanne was in driver's ed around the time this happened, and the boy's parents drilled this story into her head even before Rebecca's family moved from the country to Bardstown six months ago so that it'd be easier to get her to school and her doctor's appointments. Since then, the boy has encountered Rebecca mostly on his way to school in the morning. He walks, but she stands near the street out in front of her house and waits for the short bus to come and pick her up. Once, she called the boy over and counted from one to ten in German while staring him right in the face. Spit drooled from her mouth as she spoke the phlegmy and hard-edged words. The boy couldn't imagine a less beautiful language.

Another time, she yelled to him that she'd bought a new bikini and asked the boy if he wanted to see her try it on. When he kept his head down and his feet moving, when he didn't even swivel in the direction the words were coming from, Rebecca's voice turned mean. She shouted, "Before my accident, you would've counted yourself lucky to receive such an invitation! And I mean *lucky*!"

The next few months, she usually said something to the boy about a hot tub. She would tell him how warm the water in her hot tub was, and how good the jets would feel on his back. She would ask him if he wanted to come and sit in it with her, and then she would cackle out a broken laugh. She didn't even seem to get mad anymore when he zoomed right past her, afraid to look. Though it made no sense to him at all, it was like the shyer he became, the more fun she had goading him.

His sister, he is certain, is beautiful. She has long and wavy red hair and skin as white as the belly of a bass. It is impossible for him to imagine that Rebecca was ever beautiful the way Leanne is.

The boy stops well short of the screen door, but he can smell the mesh and dust of it. The porch is dimly lit by a window that looks in on the house proper. Rebecca, he sees, is wearing shorts.

"Name, rank, and serial number," Rebecca says.

The boy stands there smelling the door, trying not to look at Rebecca's horrible legs, thinking about how it wasn't just her face and body that were damaged in the accident. She missed an entire year of school, and they let her come back as a senior so that she could graduate, but her brain, he has heard, isn't what it used to be. He isn't sure what to say, and he feels this uncertainty as a hollowness in his throat. He starts to say his name, but Rebecca interrupts him.

"I'm kidding," she says. "Come in, come in. I'd get up, but—" She touches the tops of her metal braces. It's hard for him to believe the person sitting before him is only nineteen.

He opens the door and steps inside and smells something. It's not a bad smell, and it's strong. He can't quite identify it, and when he inhales more deeply, trying to figure it out, Rebecca points to her left. "It's eucalyptus," she says. "Look anywhere in this house, you'll probably find eucalyptus."

The door closes behind the boy. He can hear a television playing somewhere inside the house, the volume up high. He doesn't know what to do with his hands. He remembers for some reason that when he first saw Rebecca using her poles to board the school bus he thought they were kind of cool. It was like she was part robot.

"My parents fall asleep with the TV on like that every night," Rebecca says. "I come out here for some peace. Plus, it's supposed to rain sometime soon and I want to see it."

The air is humid like rain, the boy thinks, but there were no clouds in the sky earlier. "There are stars," the boy says.

"For now," Rebecca says.

The boy tries to remember whether he had seen the moon earlier. Maybe, he thinks, it was hidden by clouds.

The boy is trying not to stare, but his eyes keep flitting back and forth between Rebecca's face and her legs. He saw her face up close that one time she was shouting German—which she called Deutsch—at him like an SS officer, but all he was really seeing then were those ugly numbers. Her face, he sees now, is swollen and bumpy, puffy to the point of fat, but jagged in places, as if there is glass buried beneath the fleshy surface. Her legs aren't any better. The boy knows a little bit about skin grafts, about how doctors sometimes take skin from one part of a person's body to build up another part, and it looks like doctors have spent a lot of time gouging her legs. They're still big and jiggly-looking, but her thighs and calves are pocked with pink crevasses. The boy wishes it were darker there on the porch.

"You can sit down," Rebecca says, swiping a hand through the air at a chair across from the glider.

"OK," the boy says. He squats and sets his flashlight down near the door and then crosses the porch. The sounds coming from the TV inside are more like vibrations now. He can feel them more than he can hear them.

As the boy lowers himself into the chair, he feels his throat going dry. He thinks about those earthworms in his backyard, chugging through dry dirt, looking for mud. Once he's sitting, though, he realizes that the light over Rebecca's head is no longer illuminating her the way it was when he was outside. Now that he's closer, it's as if the two of them are sitting in almost utter darkness. All he can see of her is a vague outline, like a shadow.

"If you've come for the hot tub," Rebecca says, "I should tell you now that it's a little under the weather." She moves an arm—a thumb, maybe?—in the direction of the house. "Repair guy is supposed to come later this week."

The boy wonders whether the hot tub even exists, and he hopes, in a way that hurts, that it does. More heat lightning flashes in the sky, lighting up the porch like a camera flash, and the boy remembers how desperately Rebecca used to call out to him when he was hurrying past her on his way to school. "Hey, cutie!" she would call. "I have a hot tub! You want to come and sit with me in my hot tub?"

She had this way of leaning on her braces when she spoke. She would drape a chubby forearm over the top of one of her poles and then rise up onto the toes of her thick-soled shoes. She looked like she might topple over with want.

The boy isn't sure what to say about the hot tub. It occurs to him to say something about not having his swim trunks with him, but that seems stupid. He decides to stay quiet and sits there hoping that Rebecca asks every single boy that passes—and not just him—to come and sit with her in that hot tub that may or may not exist.

There is thunder now, and Rebecca audibly shivers. The boy's eyes are beginning to adjust, and he can see her rubbing her hands over her forearms.

"You want to sit over here?" Rebecca says. She scoots over in the glider. "You can't see what's going on out there with your back to it all."

The boy wonders whether his parents have noticed yet that he's not in the house. He remembers a time, not all that long ago, really, when his parents weren't quite so preoccupied with Leanne. Their whole family was different then. Leanne would smile, and laugh even. She talked to him. Neither one of his parents used the word "nigger" very often.

The boy stands, and Rebecca pats the glider seat with her hand. He expects her to say something pervy, to call him *loverboy* or somesuch, but she doesn't say a thing. He sits down carefully. He doesn't think he'd be strong enough to pick Rebecca up if he bumped the glider and caused her to fall to the floor.

The eucalyptus smell is even stronger now. The boy can't believe how strong it is. He takes a deep breath because the eucalyptus makes his nose tingle in a way that he likes, like sucking on a cough drop, and Rebecca catches him.

"My mom thinks the eucalyptus is going to heal me," she says. The way she says this, it sounds to the boy like she is maybe rolling her eyes.

"Really?" he says. He can't imagine a person believing a thing like this. It makes him think of witches and Indians, and these thoughts for some reason put him at ease. He lets his feet touch the floor and begins rocking the glider.

"Really," Rebecca says. "Look." She reaches down toward her shorts. They are made out of denim and fit a little tight, but she gets her fingers around the hem of one leg and begins slowly rolling it up. The boy is curious about what she's going to reveal, but he's nervous, too. He looks away.

Heat lightning flashes out on the horizon, and the sky lights up in about eighteen shades of storm, which isn't a color, the boy knows, but should be. There is real lightning, too, streaking down out of the sky in jagged, drunken bursts, as if searching, followed closely now by thunder.

"You aren't looking," Rebecca says.

When the boy glances down, she has one side of her shorts rolled up so far the skin is starting to dimple from being squeezed, and there on her thigh, as if tattooed, are little leaves.

The boy immediately reaches out to them. It's instinctual—he wants merely to touch the leaves, to see what they feel like—but he catches himself and withdraws his hand.

"It's ok," Rebecca says. "Here."

She takes hold of the boy's fingers. Her hand is warm and a little damp, and the boy's breath catches. He thinks he's lost some feeling in his fingers, that maybe they're going numb, but he lets her guide his hand.

She places it on the inside of her thigh, which is also warm and a little damp. It feels like the water balloon he left sitting out in the sun all day earlier that week. He is trying to touch her without actually touching her, but then she lifts one of his fingers and strums it across a eucalyptus leaf, from its crisp edge all the way down to its tip.

"I wear these on my skin because my mom thinks they'll make me better," Rebecca says. "I wear these *every*where."

The boy flinches and knocks one of the leaves to the floor.

Rebecca holds his hand to her leg. She is stronger than the boy'd thought. When he tries to resist, his arm won't budge. "Don't," she says. "Just relax."

The boy leans forward, hoping she won't be able to see his erection. He has woken up this way for much of the summer—his penis so stiff it aches—but if he waits long enough, if he just lies there in bed in his underwear, not moving, it usually goes away. He's not certain, though, that this will happen right now. There is something about this particular erection that feels permanent. He wishes he wasn't wearing shorts.

The boy wonders what time it is. And then he wonders what Leanne is up to, why she hasn't yet come home. He remembers hoping earlier in the night that she was missing, that she wasn't just out with Ledarius, but he wants to take back that thought now. He doesn't want to see his sister on the evening news. He doesn't want his sister to become a story that people tell like the one they tell about Rebecca.

Rebecca picks up the boy's fingers again and moves his hand down her leg to her calf. There is a divot the size and shape of a small football where doctors have taken skin at the back of her calf, and she sets his fingers inside it. The skin there is cool and completely hairless. It feels smooth in a way that skin shouldn't.

She lets go of his hand and leans back in the glider, but he keeps his fingers in the small canyon in her calf.

More lightning lights up the sky. He thinks about how high Rebecca was able to roll her shorts, and about those leaves stuck to her leg, and he begins to massage her calf with the tips of two fingers. Rebecca lets out a little moan but it might be a sigh—he isn't sure.

The boy caught his sister once, with Michael, the black guy she dated after Tony and before she started running around with Ledarius. The boy's parents were both at work, and even though they had been telling her since he was little no boys in the house during the day, she and Michael were right there in the living room, watching a movie on the good TV. Leanne gave the boy two dollars not to tell and closed him up inside his bedroom, said to call for her if he needed anything, but only if it was important. There was meanness in her face when she said this last part. There was no trace at all of the sister he'd grown up with for most of his life, and he wondered where she'd gone off to, the old Leanne. He wondered whether he would recognize her if she returned.

The boy had stayed quiet in his room for a long time. He'd ignored the sounds of the movie coming through the wall. He'd ignored his growling stomach. He'd put a pillow over his face and tried to sleep, tried to forget that there was anyone else on the planet except for him, but it was June and hot and he was sweating. He was getting thirsty.

He called for Leanne three times before he opened his door. He was curious why she hadn't answered him, sure, and he had some hazy ideas about what he might find going on in the living room, but he also wanted a drink of water. More than anything, though: He wanted his sister to remember that he was alive. When she still hadn't come to his door after the third time he'd called for her, he'd thought, What if my bedroom was on fire? What if I was dying?

He watched for what felt like a long time. Michael was on top of his sister. And then she was on top of him. The boy had the door inched open, and his throat felt raw or he might have screamed. He was hoping she both would and would not notice him standing there with one eye visible in the crack of the open door. If she noticed, he thought, maybe she'd end up feeling as terrible about that night as he was feeling. After a while, he figured that he could stand there forever and she still probably wouldn't think to come and check on him. He figured that he might as well be dead.

He closed the door and picked up his handheld video game

system and threw it against the wall, and it made a sound like a cheap toy breaking. Like nothing at all.

The boy gently digs his fingers into the skin of Rebecca's calf. It's like he is exploring her, and he takes his time. She is still leaning back in the glider, not talking but making little sounds.

He wonders — maybe because of the dark, or because of the way the walls vibrate with sounds from the TV inside, or maybe because of something else entirely — what it would be like if Rebecca was his girlfriend. If he were older and they were a couple and did the kinds of things that he knows his sister did with Michael right before he broke up with her and she started dating Ledarius. Would it be wrong for him to be with Rebecca, because she's been through such a terrible accident and now needs metal poles to help her walk around? Would it be wrong because her legs and face are gouged, the same way it's wrong for Leanne to be with black guys? If he were older, would his parents get mad at him for going with a girl like Rebecca, or would they maybe say it was OK?

The smell of eucalyptus in the room begins to weaken and the boy thinks he hears something coming from the porch roof, but he doesn't want to stop rubbing Rebecca's calf. It's like his world has become small. Manageable. Perfect.

Rebecca squirms in her seat. She rights herself. "Finally," she says. "It's raining."

The boy doesn't really want to but he unpeels his fingers from Rebecca's leg and sits back in the glider. There is no more lightning in the sky. There are no more stars. There is only rain, falling steadily but not too hard.

The air smells earthy, like something the boy's mom might force him to eat. It smells like the lake where he goes fishing. Rebecca brushes some of the eucalyptus leaves from her thigh and begins unrolling the leg of her shorts, and it's suddenly as if the two of them have been relocated to the public library, or the school cafeteria, some place where they can be strangers again. Rebecca says, "I should probably get inside now."

"Yeah," the boy says. He starts to stand but realizes he can't, not yet. "It's getting late."

He stays seated and Rebecca does too. They watch the rain fall.

They listen to it. The boy closes his eyes, and he hears behind the rain, coming from the near distance, the familiar crunch of car tires on the gravel in the alley.

Over the past few months, he has come to both love and hate this sound. He loves it because it sometimes means his sister has come home and that she will be walking in the door any minute. He hates it because sometimes—about nine times out of ten, actually—it is not his sister. It is just his mom or dad, or a neighbor. And he hates it, too, because sometimes his sister won't be alone. She will have with her Tony or Michael or Ledarius, and the boy will be like an only child all over again.

He realizes too late, because he's still a little dizzy with excitement, watching the rain, the back of his hand touching Rebecca's on the seat, that he's not hearing the crunch of gravel through his open bedroom window, the way he usually does. He realizes where he is. He sits up fast and scurries for the flashlight. He has it in his hand before he knows what he plans to do with it.

Rebecca says, "What are you doing?"

The flashlight feels heavier now than it did earlier. The crunching gravel gets louder, and the boy is certain somehow that it is his sister. He gestures with the flashlight toward Rebecca, which doesn't really answer her question, but she nods as if she understands.

"Oh," she says. She starts to say something else in that awful voice of hers, and the boy wonders if her voice was somehow damaged in the accident or if it has just gone bad—the same way she has gotten fat. The boy shows her the palm of his hand while searching the alley.

If the boy began running right now, if he shot out the porch's screen door into the rain, through the small bit of Rebecca's backyard, across the alley, and into his own backyard and up the porch steps, he could be inside his bedroom, he thinks, in seconds. In way less than a minute, at least.

More gravel crunches and headlights slash through the darkness, illuminating rain that seems to slow down as it moves through the beams of light.

A moment passes in which the boy's head is stuffed with about a thousand questions he is incapable of answering, and now the car's headlights are shining bright and white on his garage door. The garage is filled with junk—they never park the car in there. When the boy's dad said he wanted Leanne to have the car in the garage by seven, it was just an expression.

His sister puts the car in park, and the boy is trapped. There's no way he could get inside his house now without his sister seeing him.

The boy forgets all about Rebecca and gets down onto his belly. The porch floor is turf that smells like nothing and scratches his chin and knees and the bellies of his forearms.

He hears a car door open, and he thinks that maybe there's a way to turn the tables here. He inverts the flashlight so that it is pointed toward the porch floor and turns it on and off a few times, to make sure it still works, and it does: An orange-ish circle of light appears and disappears on the turf.

His eyes are so used to the darkness now he can see everything there is to see. He can see for miles.

His sister slams the car door, and behind him, Rebecca stands up out of the glider. She makes an *oomph* sound as she does this, and her metal braces clack and squeak, and the boy worries his sister will turn toward them, but she doesn't. She throws her purse over her shoulder and begins walking toward her house's back door. She is walking in her usual way—looking all slouched and grumpy and bored—and the boy turns on the flashlight but keeps it pointed toward the porch floor.

Rebecca makes it to the door that leads inside the house. She opens it and says to the boy, "Good night."

The boy waves his free hand at her, trying to shut her up. He doesn't want her to give away his location. He needs to stay hidden just a few more seconds.

Rebecca says, "Whatever," and slips inside the door without making too much noise. The television sounds rise and then fall, but still his sister makes her way slowly across the backyard toward the house in the rain, oblivious.

The boy points the flashlight's beam at the porch ceiling, to test its potency. He clears his throat.

Then he directs the flashlight toward his yard. The spot of light lands right where he wants it to, just ahead of Leanne's feet, and she leaps a little into the air. She begins looking behind her, wondering where the light is coming from, but the boy turns the flashlight off before she can locate him. Leanne puts a hand up to her eyes like she is shielding the sun and stands there in the rain like an idiot.

Then she shrugs her shoulders and starts walking again, and the boy turns the light back on and shines it in the place where her left foot is about to come in contact with the ground. Leanne turns to follow the beam, and the boy snakes the light up over her shoe. She looks down and sees the light illuminating her shoe, and the boy winds the light up her leg, and then her stomach, her chest.

Leanne puts her hands in the air, as if she is in danger of being shot. "Who's out there?" she says. "Is that you, Ledarius?" She tries to laugh but it doesn't come out right.

The boy can tell she is afraid. He moves the light from her chest to her face. She keeps her hands in the air and squints. She turns her face away but only for a second. When the boy flicks his wrist so the light hits his sister again in the chest, she says, "What do you want?"

The boy wants to keep her trapped like this by his light forever. He wants her rained on and helpless and asking questions that will never get answered.

He can feel his heart thumping against the turf floor. His breath is coming fast. He can tell by the face his sister is making, though, that she isn't going to stay there long. She is going to react to this threat in the same way she reacts to most of what the boy's parents tell her—by walking away, ignoring it. She drops her hands to her sides and looks down at the light as if it is something she can brush away with only the tips of her fingers. "I'm going inside," she says. "You can light the way if you'd like."

The boy is worried she'll recognize his voice, he's worried he won't sound intimidating enough, but he tries to make it sound like the gears churning in an enormous machine when he says, "No." When he says, "Stay where you are."

Miraculously, it works. His sister swivels toward him, her hands back in the air. The boy pins the flashlight to her chest again, and he thinks of the butterflies he pinned to a corkboard last year in school. They were so pretty and delicate, so dead and unmoving. Soon, the boy knows, his sister will be inside with his parents, and they'll be hashing things out in one way or another, but right now she is a monarch. She is a swallowtail. She is all his.

His sister looks genuinely worried. She looks afraid. She says in a trembling voice, "What do you want?"

The way she asks this simple question makes the boy falter. The light bucks on her chest. He tries to regain his confidence—he doesn't want to think about how Leanne used to be, how she would make him breakfast on the weekend when his parents slept in, how she'd read him books each night before bed—but his eyes are getting hot. He's worried he's going to cry.

"I want you to stay right there," he says. "I want you to stay right where you are."

Fostering

Haiden's morning sickness was bad, and she told
me to get the boy out of the house, take him anywhere. She stood
in the doorway of our downstairs bathroom, just off the kitchen,
her frizzy black hair bound at the top of her head and rising toward
the ceiling like a squat exclamation point. "Please," she said.

It was Saturday, the day I usually played racquetball with
friends. I twirled my racket in her direction and arched my eyebrows. "Can't you wait? I'll only be gone an hour," I said, teasing.
"No more than two."

From the living room, the boy, DeMarckus, mimicked the
sounds of Haiden's dry heaving. I imagined him kneeling over
the coffee table, his chin scrunched into his neck. The coffee table

was one of our projects from before DeMarckus had become our foster child six months earlier. Haiden and I had found the table at a garage sale, then stripped, varnished, and sandpapered the finish in spots, to give it the appearance of age. Beneath the table's beveled-glass top, we had placed a tea-stained map of the world. Listening to DeMarckus's fake heaving, I pictured the six-year-old's face hovering over the bottom half of Africa.

Haiden rolled her eyes and mouthed the words, "Take him, Rick." Out loud, she added, "Now. Like, any minute." When I hesitated, she threatened me with the back of her hand, its cinnamon skin dry and ashy.

DeMarckus's vomiting noises stopped, and he entered the kitchen and put a fist on his hip, considering Haiden. He was dressed in only a pair of backward underwear—his usual morning attire—and he tapped a bare foot on the linoleum floor and closed one eye. "Mama," he said, shaking his head, "you look like you been stepped on."

I tried to contain a laugh, wondering where the boy had gotten the line.

Haiden reentered the bathroom and shut the door, and DeMarckus stared at the spot where she had been, stretching out his neck as if to gag.

"Go get dressed, Marcky," I told him. "You and me are going to the pet store."

He eyed the racket I still had in my hand. "For real?" he said. We had been to the pet store on a couple of Saturdays, but usually in the afternoon, after racquetball.

"Totally." I set the racket on the counter. "And if you hurry, we can go get pancakes."

In seconds DeMarckus was ascending the stairs two at a time, imitating Haiden, his pretend heaves interspersed with her words, "Please. Now. Like. Any. Minute."

On Saturdays the animal shelter brought abandoned cats to the pet store in hopes of finding them homes. Just like every other time we'd been, Marcky headed straight for the back corner of the store and began naming the cats after dead presidents. The cages were tagged with the cats' real names and a short explanation for their sorry situation, but Marcky couldn't read, and even if he could, I doubt he'd have called the cats by names someone else had given them.

Hardware & Pets no longer sold hardware. The aisles that used to smell like fresh-cut lumber now had only that dirty-hamster-cage odor. Gurgling fish tanks lined every wall. I watched the boy poke his fingers through the cats' cage doors. Most of the cats were unresponsive, still sleeping off breakfast, their tails curled at the tips like genie shoes. Marcky stopped at a cage labeled SLIM: OWNERS HAD TO MOVE and said, "Eisenhower. Eisey, Eisey, Eisey. Wake up!" The fat tabby opened one eye and then must have farted, because Marcky pinched his nose and turned to me in disgust. I plugged my nose in sympathy and made a face that said, *Ewww.*

"*That* was uncalled for, Eisenhower," Marcky said, scolding the cat with his free index finger. Though his voice was nasal from the pinched nose, his tone perfectly mimicked Haiden's.

In six months of fostering DeMarckus, Haiden and I had rarely heard what the boy's real voice sounded like. He was always imitating people — their inflections and cadences, long strings of their exact words. Some of his imitations were funny. He could do the bubbly clerk from the video store: "I absolutely *love* this movie. Really. It's, like, my all-time favorite." Or my mother, while we were watching a movie: "Isn't there something more, I don't know, *useful* we could all be doing?" Other times DeMarckus's mimicry unsettled Haiden and me. Once, when I turned out the light after tucking him into bed, he said, "Oh, no. We don't cut the fucking lights out in this house. We leave the lights *on*." His voice was so cool and detached I thought there might be someone else in the room, but when I flipped on the light, I found only Marcky, angled across his bed.

I asked, "What was that?" in a voice that was equal parts anger and confusion.

Instead of answering me, Marcky said, "Thank you. That's better." He pulled the sheet over his shoulder and smushed his cheek into the pillow.

Another night, not long before she became pregnant with Ben, Haiden had just dropped hot dogs in a pan to boil when she heard a snide voice from the bathroom say, "DeMarckus? What kind of name's DeMarckus?" A feminine voice answered, "Maybe it's a black-boy name. Because he's a *black boy*." Then an unchildlike voice said, "I'll show you a fucking black-boy name, bitch."

Haiden opened the bathroom door and found Marcky staring into the mirror, his backward drawers around his knees. He quickly hoisted his drawers and jeans, ran water over his hands, and left without flushing the small turd floating in the toilet.

Later that night, during dinner, Haiden asked Marcky how school had been that day.

"Cheese pizza," he said.

Marcky often answered questions with non sequiturs about food. His favorite was "Applesauce." Haiden assumed his peculiarities were caused by two things: one, his attention deficit disorder, for which we fed him fifteen milligrams of Ritalin each morning; and two, the defense mechanisms he'd acquired during the years he'd spent with a negligent birth mother and in and out of questionable foster homes. At first she'd felt we should ignore it and give him time to adjust. But that night at dinner Haiden persisted.

"What about the other kids at school?" she asked. "How are you getting along with them?"

Marcky, his hot-dog bun covering his mouth, whispered, "Green beans." Then he rolled his eyes in feigned exasperation—an expression we found endearing—and added, "Applesauce."

Unaware of what Haiden had witnessed earlier that afternoon, I raised my hot dog high, like a scepter, and said, "Applesauce, indeed." I had expected the table to shake with laughter, but Haiden didn't laugh; instead she opened her eyes wide, as if to keep from crying. Confused but still smiling, I turned to Marcky, whose expression perfectly mirrored Haiden's.

In bed that night Haiden told me why she had been so upset. "And then you—you go and encourage him, saying 'Applesauce, indeed.'" She made a face and raised an invisible hot dog. "Do you think that's wise, Rick?" she said. "Encouraging this?"

I had no idea.

I wondered if she was maybe worried about the three of us living in Woodhull. We'd bought a big two-story house there two years earlier and were one of about six black families in town. A few black children went to the elementary school, and before we'd brought Marcky home, we'd talked to their parents, who told us things were fine, really. Not bad, anyway.

"The kids will adjust to Marcky," I told Haiden. "And he'll adjust to them."

Haiden sighed and rolled onto her side, facing away from me. It wasn't just finding him talking to the bathroom mirror, she said. It was more than that. There was something going on. "All that's happened to that boy," Haiden said. "The life he's lived . . ."

"But he's with us now," I said. "We're the life he's living." My words hung over us for a moment, but Haiden never responded. When I leaned over her to look at her face, her eyes were shut.

After Eisenhower passed gas, Marcky tapped the door of the next cage over, marked EL NIÑO: HE WAS BREAKING HIS OWNER'S HEART. A scrawny Siamese at the back of the cage sat up and began pulling himself forward using only his front paws, his lifeless hind legs dragging behind him. "Roosevelt," Marcky said, "what's wrong, boy?"

It seemed prescient of Marcky to name a cat that couldn't walk "Roosevelt." Another time he'd named an unneutered male with an erection "Kennedy." Sometimes the boy seemed to just know things.

Roosevelt collapsed with the top of his head against the cage door. "Atta boy," Marcky said. He scratched behind the cat's ears with two fingers. "You like that, don't you?" Roosevelt's front legs stiffened. "Just don't fart, OK, Mr. Roosevelt? Could you do that for me?" Marcky put his nose close to the cage and cooed, "I think you can. 'Cause you a good, no-fart kitty."

There was something about the way he said this that made me want to laugh and cry at the same time. Sometimes part of me forgot that he was just a boy, a six-year-old boy, with this tremendous capacity for empathy — for love, even.

A pretty, college-age white girl in a tight T-shirt approached and stared at Marcky, admiring the way he interacted with Roosevelt.

"Do you want to get El Niño out of his cage?" she asked, a little too eager.

Under his breath, Marcky whispered, "Pancakes."

"He's a very sweet cat," the girl said. "I think we should get him out."

Marcky turned to me, his eyes wide, and made a face like, *Can you believe this girl is talking to me?* A few months ago he would have scampered over to me and pressed his nose into my leg. I was glad to see him hanging in there for a change, trying.

The girl placed a hand on Marcky's shoulder. "Do you have any pets at home?" she asked.

"Hydrangea," Marcky said.

The girl's brow furrowed, and she looked at me. Haiden and I had a cat named Hydrangea, a fluffy white ball of fur we'd owned for almost our entire marriage. "Our cat's name is Hydrangea," I said.

The girl knelt so she was eye-level with Marcky, her palms on her thighs. "Let's get El Niño out of his cage, hmm?"

Marcky tilted his head to the side and screwed up his face as if he smelled a dirty litter pan. Then he put *his* hand on *her* shoulder while she kneeled before him, as if he were knighting or blessing her. "His name's Roosevelt," Marcky said, "and I don't think that will be necessary."

The girl stood, and Marcky's hand rose and then fell to his side. "Well, wouldn't you like to take Roosevelt home," she asked, "so Hydrangea can have a brother?"

Marcky stuck his finger in his ear, twisted it, and whispered, "Butterscotch," so low I almost had to read his lips. Then he added, out loud, in a voice that was all his, "Good-bye, Roosevelt. Good-bye, pretty girl. I love you." And he walked past me into another part of the store.

"He's a cutie," the girl said. "How old is he?"

"That kid?" I said. "I've never seen him before in my life." I chuckled, to let her in on the joke, but the girl's brow furrowed the way it had when Marcky had mentioned Hydrangea. I followed Marcky to find out where he'd gone.

About six weeks after Ben was conceived, Haiden and I sat Marcky down and explained to him that she was pregnant. I was worried about his reaction, but it turned out OK, about what I'd expect from a six-year-old: He walked over to Haiden, pointed a finger at her belly, and said, "You mean you have a baby in *there?*"

"Do you want to put your hand on my belly," Haiden asked, "to say hello to the baby?"

Marcky looked at Haiden as if a horn were protruding from her forehead. He began backing up. "No, thank you," he said. "I don't think so."

A few weeks later, though, Marcky was talking to Haiden's belly in the voice we were beginning to recognize as his, saying, "Remember, little brother or sister: Pancakes are the perfect breakfast." Or, "Don't get mad when I get to stay up later than you. You'll get to stay up late too when you're older." He was also calling Haiden "Mama" and sometimes, after I read to him from the *National Audubon Society Field Guide to North American Birds* — the kid loved birds — Marcky would call me "Dad," and I would wonder at the strange sound of it.

But there was still the problem of those voices the boy remembered from his past — the years he'd spent in foster care and being raised by a mother who'd eventually lost custody of him and his two older siblings.

Until we signed adoption papers, the caseworker couldn't tell us where he'd been and what all he might have seen before coming to us. We worried there was something predetermined about the boy's fate, no matter how much love we might give him. Even Marcky's innocent reactions — asking me, in his six-year-old voice, "For real?" or pointing at Haiden's belly and saying, "You mean you have a baby in *there?*" — sometimes seemed like an act, as if he were merely behaving the way he thought we expected him to.

I found Marcky perusing the dog toys not far from the cats' cages. Seeing me walking toward him, he pulled a five-dollar bill from his pocket, pinched the money at both ends, and snapped it twice in the air.

"Where did you get that?" I asked.

"Where do you think?" Marcky said. He huffed, and his eyes drifted toward the ceiling. "Mama gave it to me," he said. Then he held the bill out to me and asked, "How much is it?"

I pointed at one of the bill's corners. "You tell me," I said. "What number does it have on the front?" The boy couldn't read, but he knew most of his letters and all of his numbers. I guessed this was what parents did—they quizzed kids, to teach them.

Marcky disregarded my question and picked up a rubber pork chop. "Could I buy this?" he asked. "For Hydrangea. I think he deserves a treat. He's a good—"

I took the toy from him. "I asked you a question."

Marcky's lips trembled, and he started to cry. "I was just trying to do something *nice* for the kitty," he said.

The boy's tears and attempt to play innocent annoyed me. Marcky would try this at bedtime, too, or when he wanted candy, and it was simultaneously artificial and sincere, the way it is, I imagine, when most six-year-olds cry. I grabbed Marcky under his arm, and the five-dollar bill floated to the floor.

"I asked you what number was on the front of your money," I said, "and I would like for you to answer me."

My grip on Marcky's arm tightened, and I noticed the boy was on his tiptoes, real tears collecting in the corners of his eyes. I spread my fingers wide, and Marcky shrugged away from my grip and looked at the floor. In the kindest voice I could manage, I asked him to pick up the money.

Marcky bent to retrieve the bill, and when he righted himself, his tears were gone. "It's a five," he said. "ok?"

I wasn't surprised by how quickly the boy had stopped crying, but I *was* caught off guard by the strange assurance in his voice.

"I want to buy Hydrangea something," he said. "I want to spend all *five* dollars Mama gave me on Hydrangea."

"That's very generous of you," I said, "but this is the dog-toy aisle. Let's go look at the cat toys." I put my arm around Marcky's shoulder, and he pressed his head into my side.

"Yeah, yeah," he said, "very generous of me."

———————

Haiden's getting pregnant with Ben after Marcky came to live with us wasn't something we planned. We had tried for three years to have a child—three years without doctors. Then, rather than seek a medical explanation for our difficulties, we registered to become foster parents.

Before Marcky came to live with us, his caseworker told us the boy was "SACY," an acronym that stood for "sexually aggressive children and youth," which we were told didn't mean that the boy was a preschool sex offender; he just knew more than most kids his age about sex. We had to notify the school when we registered him for first grade, and the principal said they'd handled SACY kids before. They just had to keep an eye on him around the other students. Nothing out of the ordinary.

Haiden and I knew there had to be reasons for this designation, but those reasons were locked inside Marcky's six-year-old head, and in a file his caseworker kept, which we would be allowed to access only after the adoption took place—if it took place. Haiden and I tried to find out what he had been exposed to, so we could know what we were dealing with, but the caseworker said the information was "sensitive." It included police and psychiatric reports and the names of other foster parents and details about what had happened in their homes. There was no way, the caseworker said, that she could present that kind of information to people who might choose to maintain custody of the boy for only a day or so.

Haiden and I were OK with this at first; we didn't think there was anything we could find out that would make us not want to take Marcky into our home.

And then Haiden got pregnant.

When we told the caseworker, she seemed almost alarmed. "OK," she said. "There are ways to handle this. It isn't anything to get worked up about."

We hadn't known that it might be, and all this secrecy was beginning to get to us. We asked just what was in that file. "Just tell us," I said. "Let us know."

Without giving any details, the woman said that Marcky might be better off in a home without any other children around. She said it could work out all right, though, that often there are no problems at all.

But that wall of doubts the caseworker had erected around Marcky was enough. If it had just been the three of us—Haiden, Marcky, and me—I think we could have made it work. But it wasn't going to be just us three.

We told DeMarckus's caseworker we would keep the boy for now, until she found another suitable foster home, but that, after thinking it through, we weren't going to adopt.

For Hydrangea, Marcky picked out two realistic-looking brown mice filled with catnip and handed them to me along with his five-dollar bill. "You pay," he said.

While the storeowner rang up the mice, Marcky stood by my side and drummed his fingers on the counter. "Excuse me, lady," he said. I thought maybe he wanted to tell her about Hydrangea or let her know he was paying for these gifts with his own money. But Marcky looked concerned.

"Yes, young man?" the storeowner asked.

"Those cats back there," Marcky said. He pointed toward the back of the store. "Where do they live when it isn't Saturday?"

The woman smiled and said, "Well, their real house is the animal shelter."

"Then what?" Marcky said.

The storeowner turned to me, and I shrugged, as if to say, *Are six-year-olds supposed to know about the mechanics of animal shelters?*

"Well—"

Marcky stopped her. "I don't want the mice," he said. "I want to give all my money to the kitties."

"Oh, honey," the woman said. "I don't think—"

"To the kitties," he said. "All five dollars."

I reached out to put my arm around Marcky, but he pulled his shoulder away from my hand. I had never seen the boy so serious-looking. "All I want is to give the money to the cats," he said. "Maybe especially Roosevelt."

On previous trips to the store, I had entertained the idea that Marcky had an intuition about the animals' plight, but the boy's interest in the cats had always seemed uncomplicated, as if he liked them more for their catness than anything else, the way any kid would.

But this, this felt different.

"All right," I told him. "It's your money."

The storeowner asked us to wait, and she snagged the college girl, who brought out a marker and a donation sheet shaped like a cat's paw. Marcky placed the paw on the store's counter, and I spelled out his name for him, one letter at a time. Meanwhile, the storeowner produced a Polaroid camera to take our picture.

In the photos Haiden and I have of Marcky, he is only half-smiling, as if he has just asked a question and received an answer he doesn't understand. When I look at those pictures now, I smell the boy's bad morning breath; I see the streaks of toothpaste he used to leave in the sink.

The college girl stood behind Marcky, bent at the waist, and placed both her hands on his shoulders. I tried to slink out of the shot while the storeowner looked through the camera's viewfinder.

"Oh, no," she said. "Get back there, you."

I stood behind them and off to the side, just barely caught by the camera's flash. The storeowner took two pictures, one to attach to the cat's paw Marcky had signed, and one for us to have as a keepsake.

On the drive home from the pet store, Marcky fiddled with the window button and asked his typical questions, like "Do flowers have feelings?" or "Superman isn't *really* a man, right?" I tried to answer his questions as best I could, but my head was filled with, *All I want is to give the money to the cats. Maybe especially Roosevelt.*

When we made it home, Haiden was in the kitchen making a salad, and all signs of sickness had left her face. Marcky bounded through the kitchen on his way to the television. The Polaroid, I would find out later, was still in the car, where Marcky had dropped it.

"How was your trip to the pet store?" Haiden asked as she halved a handful of grape tomatoes and tossed them in a bowl.

"Well," I said, "it looks like we have a hero down at Hardware & Pets."

Haiden, of course, had no way of knowing what I meant, but she placed her knife on the counter, smiled, and said, "Come here."

And I held her there in the kitchen, with the bump of Ben between us. We were so isolated, yet so together right then. We held
one another and didn't let go, and it felt like we were waiting: For
Marcky to gag over the coffee table. For him to say, "Applesauce."
For anything from him at all.

The Woodlands

When she said that it was just her and her birds — that her apartment was like a zoo, only she didn't even keep the things caged all the time — maybe he shouldn't have told her that his mom owns a pair of cockatiels. Maybe he shouldn't have told her about the time he visited his mom a few months earlier, and how while she worked during the day, he stayed down in the basement with the television on mute, listening to her birds whistle the theme song from *The Andy Griffith Show* from upstairs, over and over.

The woman was already drunk, and he was just there for a nightcap. Sitting on the bar's deck, looking out over the man-made lake attached to the main building of the resort he was staying at in The Woodlands, Texas. The crowd had scattered, and the woman's left eye was slurring closed each time she took a breath. The left side of her mouth sagged when she tried to smile.

"A lot of cockatiels know that song," she said. She was sitting down at his table now, and she seemed to list without moving. "You have to work with them, though, and I don't get the chance to work with mine anymore. Too many of them."

He didn't tell her that since his divorce he had been staying with his mom pretty much whenever he wasn't on the road, working as a corporate technology trainer. For the past three days, he'd been in Texas showing pharmaceutical sales representatives how to operate their new customer interface systems. He didn't tell the woman that he was thirty-six years old and that listening to his mom's cockatiels from the basement as they sang that song was one of the loneliest things he'd ever heard. And he hadn't heard it just once. He heard the song every morning he wasn't on the road, and the birds usually sang for hours. The woman seemed too sad, too desperate, so he'd lied a little. He knew that if he mentioned the divorce, or if he told her what he felt every time he heard that song, the two birds singing slightly out of sync and off-key, the woman may have loved him forever.

She was at the resort for some chamber of commerce cocktail hour, which was beginning to wind down when he showed up. He had seen the welcome sign in the lobby and then taken a seat alone at a table looking out over the lake. He noticed the woman almost immediately. She had a wide face and dull brown hair. Her arms seemed a little too long for her thin body. He wasn't attracted to her at all, but he couldn't stop watching her as she tried to schmooze. The other people at the party were better looking and better dressed than she was, and every time she tried to join a conversation circle, the people seemed instinctually to close her out of it. But still she stumbled around trying, sticking out her chin toward a group of people here and there, laughing a few seconds later than the rest of them at some joke. It pained him to watch her trying to fit in like that, and he didn't look away until he had been staring for a long, rude time.

The woman leaned onto the table now and said that there was a bar not far from there where the drinks were cheaper. "Do you know what they're charging inside for a bottle of Corona?"

Her drooping eye and mouth, he realized, weren't from drunkenness. She was without a doubt drunk but those parts of her face seemed dead, unmuscled, and he was betting she'd had Bell's palsy at some point in her life. His aunt had suffered Bell's palsy a few years earlier. She woke up one morning alone in her bed, not knowing anything was wrong, and minutes later, she didn't recognize her own face in the bathroom mirror. Over time, the nerve damage healed and her face returned to normal, but sometimes, when she got tired, he could see the hint of how her face had looked back then.

He told the woman that he had an early flight out of town the next morning, that his room was nearby. "I should probably get to bed sometime soon," he said.

The woman scratched the table with her thumbnail, working at something crusty. When she looked up, she said, "But I want to show you my birds. The ones I told you about."

Earlier, when he was trying to force himself not to watch this woman, he would focus on a line of trees, backlit by the setting sun, on the far side of the lake. The trees were just a few hundred yards away, and he could see white spots filling one of the tree's branches. He'd thought the spots were only gaps in the tree's leaves, but he couldn't understand why those gaps didn't orange and pink when the sun was setting, when the sky all around the tree was changing color, deepening. After he'd forgotten about the spots in the tree for a while, he looked at them again, and one of them started moving. Then another one moved, and another. In just moments, dozens of large white birds erupted from the tree. They flew up into the air, circling, and then settled again.

For the past hour, he had been wanting to feel what he felt when he saw that first bird move, when he saw the flock of them converge on the sky, spreading their wide white wings.

The woman looked at him expectantly with her slightly drooping face.

"How many cockatiels did you say you owned?" he asked.

Her face brightened. "Twelve," she said. "Only three of them have names, though."

It was a short walk to her apartment, past a strip mall, a chain restaurant. The woman didn't talk much, and he was glad. All he wanted was to give her this thing—this moment of attention, this acknowledgment—and then get back to the resort. When they reached her door, the woman opened it only slightly, then turned to him as he stood there on her straw welcome mat, and fell into his arms. She began to nuzzle at the side of his neck with dry lips.

He didn't want this, not at all, but he didn't want to humiliate the woman either. He held her for a moment, staring at the open door, trying to figure out a way to keep from stepping through it. The woman smelled like dust and the limes his mom liked to slice into wedges for the vodka tonics they would drink together some nights in her kitchen.

The woman's dry lips against his neck felt good, really—warm. The feeling reminded him for some reason of kissing his wife after they had both been crying and were beginning to make up, to come back together again.

He locked his hands behind the small of the woman's back and held her to him. A part of him wanted to encourage her to keep kissing his neck the way she was, and another part of him wanted to keep her from pulling away from him, to keep her from looking up into his eyes with expectation.

She stopped kissing him and pressed the side of her face against his chest, settled against him. His hands were still behind her back, and he knew that soon the woman was going to break their embrace. She was going to pull away from him and then take him by the hand and lead him through her apartment door.

He had been imagining a moment like this for the past three years. Every time he went on the road, even when he was still married. Only he would imagine his seducer as one of the pharmaceutical reps he usually trained, as one of the smiling and beautiful, the confident. For a moment, he imagined the woman in his arms was not this woman at all. He imagined she was Shelly, a blond with big bangs and pretty feet from Dallas whom he had been training for the past three days. He imagined the way Shelly smelled when he would lean over her laptop to show her how to access the drop menu she would need to click on before she collected a doctor's electronic signature. He imagined the way Shelly would smack herself on the forehead and laugh, the way she would touch his forearm with her manicured nails before he moved on to the next person with a question.

Still, he knew that even if this were Shelly he was holding, even if this were Shelly breathing softly against his chest, he would be no less terrified.

The woman's breath was even, almost rhythmical, and he wondered if maybe she would fall asleep standing, right there in his arms. He imagined the relief he would feel then, helping her inside, tucking her into bed, walking back to the resort.

The woman began to slide her hands slowly up and down his back. She used the tips of her fingernails, and it sent spiders crawling up his spine. It felt good in places her hands did not even touch, were nowhere near touching.

His eyes closed, and he leaned into the woman so that she would keep doing what she was doing. It occurred to him that he wouldn't mind it if she kept scratching his back until he fell asleep, until he had slept for days. Those spiders beneath his skin were building a web now — magnificent, intricately designed, silky.

Maybe, he thought, he *should* have told this woman about his mom's cockatiels and the song they sang. Maybe he should have even told her about his divorce.

At one time, before the man-made lake was built, before there were thirty-six holes of golf to play, the resort he'd been staying at was actual woodlands. Fir, spruce. Everywhere. There was no bar with an attached deck. There were no snowy egrets roosting. The land was untouched. Uncultivated. A PC without any hardware.

He was thinking of the place they had just left as it had been back then — full of potential, waiting — when he heard the first bird whistle. And he was still thinking of it when he heard a second bird squawk. Then another whistle. His eyes opened, and the woman was still there against his chest, breathing evenly, running her nails up and down his back, and from behind her, through the open door, he heard wings beating. He heard a chorus of birds getting louder, whistling, beginning to sing a song that was not a song.

Peloma

My twelve-year-old daughter Peloma kept trying to kill herself.

She tried three times, two years after my wife, Marcella, died in a car accident. The first two were kind of pathetic attempts, but still.

I blamed the counselors and myself. The counselors kept telling her that her mother was in a better place, that what was important was how Peloma lived her life right now, and that she remembered her mother, and was happy; me, I went on and on about the afterlife. Peloma was smart, though. She knew better. But then she decided to hurry to that better place, where dead folks sing and walk on clouds and her mother wears large white wings and a halo as round and gold and perfect as the wedding band I still kept attached to my finger.

The first time she tried to kill herself, Peloma took seven aspirin and lay in a bathtub full of lukewarm water. She wrote a note, and when I got home from the steel factory at five I found it taped to the seat of my recliner. It said: Dad, I took seven aspirin. Love, Pell.

As a part of my new position at Peterson Steel, I had to run two shot peen tumblers. I put small iron springs and Belleville washers into the tumblers where shot peen—tiny steel balls—pummeled the pieces until they were bright silver, shiny as new dimes. The machines did all of the work, which was nice, but I came home covered in shot peen pellets every day. When I opened the tumbler doors the tiny pieces of metal sprayed all over the place, like they were trying to make me as shiny as the steel. Reading that note, I felt like I'd just spent fifteen minutes inside a tumbler and someone had jerked open the door before the cycle was up.

I rushed into the bathroom and found Pell sitting on the toilet with a towel wrapped around her shoulders, shivering. The tub was full of clear water, and shot peen fell from my work boots into the puddles Pell had dripped onto the linoleum. I grabbed a dry towel, wrapped it around Pell's shoulders, and held her so close to my chest my jacket left a quench oil stain on her forehead.

Pell looked up at me and said, "It didn't work." I started to say something back to her, her name, "P—," but she stood up and dwarfed me.

At twelve, Pell was almost six feet tall and weighed close to two hundred pounds. That was the other thing I blamed for her suicide attempts: puberty. Puberty hit Pell early, just after she turned ten, just after her mother's car hit a pickup truck head-on at the top of a hill. I thought of what was going on inside Pell's body as a head-on collision between a sweet awkward child and buckets of hormones, which, like carbon monoxide, you cannot touch, taste, or smell. You could see the effects of the things on Pell's body, though. Before, she was big-boned and orange-haired, like Marcella. Then her breasts and her hips and her everything grew so that same orange hair was on top of a body that I'm sure the kids called fat, though I'd say was full-figured, like her mother's.

By the time Pell and I stopped making monthly trips to the

mall for larger bras and I'd already warned her ten to twelve times about the dangers of toxic shock syndrome (Pell insisted on tampons, said pads were for "girls," and I'd locked myself in the bathroom one night and studied the diagrams and the warnings that came packaged inside each little blue box), she was five inches or so taller than me and outweighed me by about seventy pounds. Less than a year after Marcella was gone, her physical double had appeared, though the new Marcella was clumsy, distrustful, and afraid of the new body she'd been given.

I had taught Pell about cup sizes and how a tampon applicator works, but I still wasn't comfortable being a single parent, and I didn't know what to do about a suicide attempt. So that night I made chicken noodle soup and grilled cheese sandwiches. Pell ate a little, taking small bites, scraping her spoon against the bottom of her soup bowl, and then said she was going to bed. I tucked her in, half-shut her bedroom door, and walked back out to my recliner. Pell's note was still on the seat.

I thought about calling Donna, the counselor Peloma saw the summer Marcella died, but I figured that would only make things worse. Pell hated Donna. All Donna ever did during their sessions was ask Pell how she felt that day, on a scale from one to ten. Pell and I would joke about it on the way home. She would pretend to be all serious, clasping her pearl-white hands in front of her, saying, "Tell me, Dad, how *are* you feeling today? How are *you* feeling today? No. How are you *feeling* today?"

Early in the summer, Pell would tell Donna, "Five, five-and-a-half." As the weeks wore on, Pell's number slowly rose, and her counselor decided we could discontinue the sessions. Like I said, Pell's a smart girl.

The night she swallowed seven aspirin I slept on and off and sneaked down to her room every half hour just to listen to her breathe through the half-shut door. In the morning, I made a big breakfast for her and left for work while she was still in the shower. I wrote a note and left it under her silverware, next to the plate of eggs and toast and sausages. It said: On a scale from one to ten, how are you feeling today? Love, Dad.

I was crazy worried about Pell that day, and I was having my own problems at work, too. I had worked in Plant Two at Peterson

Steel, making hot-coiled springs, for fifteen years, but just before Marcella died I'd earned an associate's at the junior college, thinking I'd maybe find somewhere to work where I didn't come home covered in oil and tiny steel balls. One of the stiff-collars got word I'd put two years of college under my belt and decided they could save some money by moving me into the quality-control position they'd just invented for Plant Two. Plant Two was four blocks from the other three plants that made up Peterson Steel, and the stiff-collars were tired of having to move the springs around to get them tested. The bosses had thought they were going to have to pay some degree a serious salary to take the position, but instead, they offered me a one-dollar-per-hour pay raise to take it up.

I balked a little, but the bosses didn't give me much of a choice. They brought a bunch of equipment down to Plant Two from up the hill at Plant One, and some twenty-four-year-old tie-wearing degree showed me how to use it. Before, we had gotten reports from and bitched about some nameless guy up the hill who decided our springs were shit. Now I had to do the tests and tell the guys I'd worked with for fifteen years that their Rockwell was off or their resistance was too tight, that they had to run another set of testers. Plus they put me in charge of those shot peen tumblers, which was a job usually reserved for someone on light-duty because of a back injury from dealing with the big jobs.

I'd never been one to say much on breaks, when we all sat around on empty upside-down paint buckets and stared out the open bay door at people driving by on the street. Once Marcella died and I became the asshole who told the guys they had to redo everything they'd already done, they started ignoring me completely, and not too long after that, I was tired of being the asshole. I was tired of the silence that followed me around all day at work. The morning after Pell swallowed seven aspirin, I decided that I was going to lie and say that every spring I tested was perfect.

I collected sample springs all that day and returned them to the guys with the go-ahead on the run. Most of the guys didn't say much, but I could tell they were surprised. They raised eyebrows, looked at me sideways.

Toward the end of the day I collected two brake pad springs Jackson was working on for an important job. The stiff-collars were talking seven, eight million dollars if we got the contract. They were going to expand Plant Two and set up machines that ran only the brake pad springs for two full shifts a day.

When I'd finished the tests I carried them over to Jackson, who was tweaking the brake spring press with an Allen wrench. He saw me coming his way and looked like he didn't want to hear what I was going to tell him. In truth, the ends weren't square on the two I'd tested; they wobbled when I stood them on end—the press was bending the steel. And the machine said the Rockwell was off—the springs were too brittle—but I didn't care.

"They're right in the middle on everything," I said. "Hardness, length, everything. You're ready to roll."

"No shit," Jackson said. He let out a hearty scoff and tossed the Allen wrench into a small pile of shot peen at the foot of the press.

"No shit," I said. And then: "Fucking run 'em."

Word spread about the run of good springs, and when we went to clock out at four-thirty, a few of the guys asked me how Peloma was doing. They'd seen her at company picnics when Marcella was still alive and probably guessed Pell wasn't terribly athletic or popular at school, but they asked anyway.

"She just started taking piano lessons," I lied. "And I guess she's some kind of virtuoso. Her teacher says she's gifted."

"Well, fuck, Clem," they said. "You always said she was a smart one."

I walked out of Plant Two that day with a smile on my face, and when I got home, Pell had a meatloaf in the oven and the table set. She stood at the oven door wearing a pink apron that was too small for her, the way it had been for Marcella, and when she saw me, she said, "About a five, a five-and-a-half."

I shook pieces of metal off my clothes and showered while the meatloaf finished cooking. It felt good to hear the shot peen pellets fall from my ears and nose and butt crack and plink on the tub's porcelain. I even used Pell's loofah to get at the quench oil lodged under my fingernails. I shaved and dressed in clean clothes and had dinner with my daughter, who wore the too small pink apron while we ate, and then asked me if I wouldn't mind cleaning up because she had some homework to do, to which I replied, "No. No. I wouldn't mind cleaning up at all."

At home, all that week, I left notes asking, "On a scale from one to ten . . ." beside Pell's breakfast plate, and when I came home, she had dinner ready and had raised her self-ranking half a number.

At work, bars of steel were heated in two thousand–degree fires and coiled by men or machines into springs. These springs were dipped in quench oil to cool and temper the metal, and then hardened in long ovens, and sent through the shot peener. The springs were then pressed and picked up by me for testing, and I gave the go-ahead on every set of testers I touched. Everyone was happy. When we punched out at the end of the day, I told the guys more stories about Peloma's piano abilities, how her teacher was thinking a concert was in order. And, sure, I'd invite every one of them if they felt up to coming. We could all hear her play.

Then, seven days after her first suicide attempt, I came home from work and didn't smell anything cooking in the oven. There was another note taped to the seat of my recliner. It said: Dad, I'm off the scale. Love, Pell. I headed straight for the bathroom and found her there on the floor in her pink apron, her arms stretched toward the toilet. She had nicked her wrist with the paring knife that lay near her hand; a half-dollar of blood pooled beside it. Her eyes were closed like she was sleeping, and water was running in the tub, but Pell hadn't used the drain plug, so the water just splashed into a small puddle and continued down the drain and into the pipes.

I shook Pell's shoulder as if I were trying to wake her after she'd fallen asleep in the car on a long trip, and she sat up. Her orange hair was matted where it had been pressed against the linoleum. "I must have passed out," she said.

I held her, pulling her face toward the same quench oil stain on my jacket that had marked her forehead a week ago, knowing I was going to have to call Donna. But first, I found the bandages over the sink, next to the blue box of tampons, and dressed the small wound on Pell's wrist with antibiotic and a square of gauze. Then I made tomato soup and grilled tuna salad sandwiches. We ate, and Pell went to bed early.

Once I could tell Pell was asleep I called Donna at her home number, which I got from an automated directory at the mental health center. I told her what had happened, and she insisted on coming over right then.

I showered quickly, thinking the whole time about Pell the summer after Marcella died, how she would fold her hands and ask, "No. How are you *feeling* today?" I wished I could close my ears to shut out the sounds the shot peen made when it landed in the tub. I tried to picture the woman sitting across the desk from Pell that summer, but it was useless; I had never actually met Donna. The people at the mental health center said they liked to work with children without interference from the parents whenever possible, and I didn't see any reason to object.

I dressed in a pair of blue jeans and a T-shirt and waited for Donna on the front porch, where I ran my thumbs over the tips of my fingernails, still mucked up with oil. A few minutes later, Donna pulled up in a Saturn. She was a short, stout woman with curly brown hair and large eyeglasses, and she wore a dress and low pumps that made her calves look heavy. I met her halfway down the sidewalk, between the house and the street.

She whispered and cupped her hand at the side of her mouth, like she didn't want the neighbors to hear, when she asked, "Where is Peloma now?"

"She's inside the house." I whispered, too. I almost cupped my hand to my mouth but caught myself.

"How is she doing?" Donna asked.

"She's sleeping. She ate some dinner, though." A light wind blew, and Donna shivered. A few leaves fell from the trees.

"Good, good," she said. She looked around at our neighbors' houses, keeping her hand near her mouth while she talked. She wanted details about Pell's suicide attempt that night.

I described the cut, how she was lying on the floor when I got there, the tub trying to fill with water. Then I brought up the seven aspirin, and Donna's hand dropped, her voice grew loud.

"She tried this last week?" She raised her hand again as a shield. "You definitely should have called me." She went on about how unusual this was for someone Pell's age. She reeled off some statistics and recommended we admit Pell to a treatment facility in Indianapolis, an hour south.

I didn't like the idea. I asked Donna to come by in the morning so we could discuss it with Pell face-to-face, and she agreed, telling me to take care of myself, to get some rest, she'd see me in the morning.

I didn't sleep at all that night. I sat in the dark and wished hard that Marcella were around. I wanted to ask her how she dealt with puberty when she was Pell's age. I wanted to know how she'd acquired the confidence she had when I'd met her and how I could help give that same confidence to Peloma. I wanted to ask her what she knew about dealing with loss and grief.

I called in sick to work in the morning and made waffles and bacon for Pell's breakfast. Donna rang the doorbell while Pell was still in the shower.

Right away Donna started talking about a court order and late-night phone calls, about how Pell was going with her to Indianapolis.

"It's seven-thirty in the morning," I said.

"Everything is already set. They just want to observe her at the facility for a week or so. It'll be fine, Clem."

When she saw Donna, Pell stopped in the hallway on her way to the kitchen, and Donna walked toward her. "Good morning, sweetie," she said. It looked like the counselor was going to try to hug her.

"Dad," Pell said.

I told her it was all for the best, that Donna was going to help her, that she wouldn't have to stay long in Indianapolis.

Pell didn't cry or throw a fit or anything the way you'd expect a twelve-year-old to. She just walked back to her room and packed a bag. While she was gone I asked Donna if I could come along for the ride, and she said I could but that once Pell was admitted at intake I wouldn't be able to see her until six o'clock that night.

I thought maybe I should give Peloma an hour alone with Donna in the car and some time at the facility without me around, so I walked back to Pell's room and told her I would visit her that night in Indianapolis, and that she should be good, and listen to what the counselors had to say, that I wanted her to get better. Pell packed her bag without looking at me. Her hair was pulled back in a ponytail, and still wet, and she left a trail of shampoo scent in the hallway, all the way to the door, where Donna reached up and put her hand on Pell's shoulder. They walked down the sidewalk that way—Pell's bag banging absently against the back of her leg—to Donna's car, and they were gone.

For five days, I called in sick to work, and for five nights, I visited Pell in Indianapolis. Each time I went, a man dressed in khaki pants and a button-up shirt walked her to the visitation room, where we were left alone. I feigned seriousness each night, and said, "On a scale from one to ten, ten being the highest, the best . . ."

Pell laughed, every time. The place was clean, and Pell didn't complain about anything except for wanting to come home. It was the same trick, she said, of making them believe she was feeling better. I wanted to know if she actually was feeling better, but I figured that if she wanted to come home, then, well, maybe she was doing all right. So I didn't tell her not to lie to the counselors, but I did tell her to listen to them, and that I hoped she really was feeling better.

On the sixth day Pell had been gone, about an hour before I left to visit her, Donna called and said she was bringing my daughter home. I would have her back in two hours.

I decided to put Pell's room in order before she and Donna arrived. The room wasn't dirty, but I fluffed the pillows on her bed and hung clean clothes in her closet. I dusted her dresser and straightened the wooden jewelry box that had belonged to Marcella, and the tiny glass figures Pell kept on top of it.

I was putting away her clean bras and underwear when I found the opened envelope with the card inside. The envelope was addressed to Pell in block letters; there was no return address. I didn't think I should open it, but I didn't know of anyone who would send Peloma a card.

The outside of the card was navy blue and gold, covered with stars and half-moons. On the inside, the card read: Why are you still alive?

I don't think the people who made the card intended for the message to be mean. I think it was supposed to be life affirming in some way. More like: There is a reason you are still alive. What is it? Now go out and do that. But it wasn't the kind of card you sent an overweight, suicidal twelve-year-old.

I went to slide the card back and found a whole stack of them behind a wall of crumpled underwear. Each envelope was addressed to Peloma in the same handwriting, and each contained the same exact card. Not one of the cards was signed, and not one of the envelopes had a return address. I looked at each card and each identical message, trying to figure out who was sending them and why they would do such a thing, until I heard a knock at the door.

Then I restacked the cards, stuffed them into the drawer, and ran down the hallway to the living room. Pell rolled her eyes in Donna's direction and carried her bag to her room. Donna was all smiles. She motioned for me to join her on the front porch.

"I think this has been the best thing for Peloma," she said. "She says she's feeling wonderful. That it was just a rough patch and now she's through it."

I spoke loudly, so maybe Pell would hear me and appreciate Donna and Donna's help the way I seemed to. "That's great. Really. You've been such a help." I put my hand on her back to get her going toward her car.

"Let me tell Peloma good-bye," she said.

"I'll be right here."

I stood there wondering when all the leaves on the trees had fallen. The yard around me was full of them, but I couldn't imagine when it had happened.

I thought that maybe I could ask Donna for some answers about Pell, some real answers, not just the same self-evaluation responses that Pell had been giving her. I wondered if I should tell Donna about the cards Pell had been receiving, if she would want to discuss them with her. Then I figured that if Donna had the kind of answers I was looking for, she wouldn't be working as a counselor for the mental health center. She would be writing books and making television appearances. She wouldn't be Donna at all.

Donna exited the house more chipper than ever. "The doll's asleep," she said. "Good night, Clem."

I waved her out of the neighborhood, and once I was inside, I checked on Pell. She was asleep, still in her clothes, on top of the comforter. I told her good night from the hallway and half-closed her door.

The next morning I made omelets with everything and toast. I wrote the same note, "On a scale from one to ten . . ." and placed it under Pell's silverware. I waited for her to get out of the shower, told her to have a good day, and I left for work.

Jackson stopped me outside the door to Plant Two. I thought maybe he was going to ask about my illness, see if I was feeling okay. "What the fuck, Clem?" he said. "They sent back those brake springs every day last week. Snapped in half. Been at least twenty of 'em dropped off in your office."

"They were fine when I tested them," I said. "They passed specs."

"Well, we already got ours," he said. "They've been waiting to give you yours."

The stiff-collars came down from Plant One with the twenty-four-year-old after lunch. They checked the calibrations on my machines with some of the springs that hadn't snapped, the "good ones." The "good ones" hadn't broken, but they were bent into crooked letters and question marks.

The twenty-four-year-old told me that the springs were a mess and asked what I'd been doing down here.

"What *have you* been doing down here?" the stiff-collar said.

"I've been out for the last week," I said. "Sick."

They explained that the run they'd had painted and performance-tested were from a few weeks ago, when I was still working.

"Then I have no idea what's wrong with those springs," I said. "I haven't got a clue."

"Why don't you take the afternoon off," the stiff-collar said. "We'll get back to you."

At home, I found another envelope for Peloma in the mail. It was in the same handwriting as the others, without a return address. I threw it in the trash can and started an early dinner.

When Peloma got home she said, "A six, a six-and-a-half." We ate. She did the dishes.

The rest of the week went well. I left notes for Pell, and her self-rating improved daily. She made dinner, and I washed the dishes while she did her homework. At work, they discovered the power had gone out one night a few weeks earlier during second shift. The stiff-collars ran some numbers and were guessing that the springs in the K-30 furnace, where they're heat-treated after the quench oil application, were baked brittle while the furnace cooled during the power outage. I was off the hook.

The morning of the day Peloma attempted suicide for the third time, the stiff-collars came to see me again. They'd received another shipment of broken springs.

"I don't know what to tell you," I said.

"Think about your job here," the stiff-collar said. He went on about how they probably couldn't fire me because of the union but they could make my job a lot less fun.

I whistled for the rest of the day. I even stopped at the press for a while and helped Jackson put some brake springs into boxes. I didn't test a single one of them. The thing about those brake pad springs, they were for tractor-trailers, and the way they were installed, they didn't do much of anything until the real brakes quit working. Then something—I don't even know what—kicked in and snapped the spring so the truck could come to a stop. So the springs, they were supposed to break, eventually; they only had to remain intact until they were needed as a safety.

While we were clocking out, the guys were appreciative of my lack of effort, even if they'd had their butts chewed. They knew their jobs were safe. The pride of that big contract was more a luxury for the guys who signed the paper than anybody else.

I told them that Pell and I were planning the concert, that we were having tickets made. They were going to have to pay to see my virtuoso play. Everyone laughed.

At home, I took my jacket off and shook the shot peen out of it on the front porch, and inside, there was no sign of Peloma. On my chair, another note read: Dad, I'm on the roof. Love, Pell.

Behind the house, the ladder was leaned up against the gutter. I climbed up and found Peloma standing beside the chimney, which was made of bricks almost the color of her hair.

We were one story, maybe twelve feet, off the ground.

I didn't know what to say to Pell, but I was glad I got to her before she jumped off the roof and twisted her ankle or sprained her knee. "Come on, Pell," I tried. "Let's go inside."

"I'm going to jump, Dad," she said. "And you can't stop me." Gooseflesh covered her arms up to her elbows.

"You're right," I said. "I can't really stop you."

Pell walked gingerly down the slope of the roof toward the gutter, which was filled with wet leaves. I followed her down, and then squatted and began pulling out handfuls of leaves and throwing them onto the ground.

"You could help me out with this," I said. I kept throwing wet leaves onto the blanket of newly dead ones that surrounded the house, and Pell did the same. She was careful not to lose her balance when she squatted at the edge of the roof, and she removed the leaves and tossed them confidently to the ground.

We worked our way around all four gutters, not saying anything to one another, and when the gutters were clean, Pell seemed to remember her reason for being on the roof. She walked to the side we'd begun cleaning on and stood with her toes hanging over the gutter.

"Nice trick, Dad," she said. "But I'm still going to do it."

I hadn't been on the roof of our house for a long time. We weren't high off the ground, but I could still see quite a ways. I saw Peloma's elementary school and her junior high, where she had quit writing in cursive in favor of block letters. And I thought about those block letters, how they always bent toward the left side of the page, how they didn't quite stand up straight, like those springs without squared ends. I could see the high school Pell would go to in a few years, too, and the roofs of my neighbors' houses and the inner branches of trees, where birds had abandoned their nests.

"Let's take the ladder down," I said. "We'll probably fall off one of the rungs anyway."

When she didn't say anything, I walked over to her. She told me to stop or else.

I stood beside her. She shook from the knees up, told me not to come any closer. It was a short distance to the ground, really. I could see the veins in the dry red and orange leaves down there.

"I mean it," she said.

I took her hand. Her fingers trembled against mine, and my fingers trembled a little against hers, too.

I squeezed her hand and let out a slow breath, like when I would slide open one of the shot peen tumblers, just before I pulled out the shiny springs.

And together, we jumped.

Let x

Let x equal the moment just after he tells her he's starting a club for people who know something about computers.

It is summer, 1984, and this is their grade school playground. She is idling on a swing over a patch of scuffed earth. He stands just off to the side, one hand on the chain of the swing next to hers.

Let y equal her laughter. Her laughter sounds like a prank phone call at three A.M. It sounds a little evil.

She throws her head back, and even though he is hearing the

y of her laughter in the wake of that moment *x*, he can't stop staring at her hair. He can't believe how black, how shiny, how perfect it is.

She stands up out of the swing and asks, "What do you know about computers?"

It is 1984. Nobody at this elementary school—or in Monmouth, Illinois, in general—knows all that much about computers.

Let *z* equal the face he makes. The face is not a reaction to her question but to her laughter.

He was trying to impress her with this computer club. He knows she is smarter than he is. He knows that she was, in fact, smarter than everyone in the entire fifth grade, and that next year, when they start pre-algebra, she will be the smartest person in the sixth grade, too.

He can't help the *z* of his face. He feels humiliated. His ears are tiny fires, and her hair and face, both of which he finds beautiful, has always found beautiful, are beginning to blur together. She has stopped laughing, but he can still hear the ghost of it as he searches for a variable that might make it as if none of this ever happened.

In a moment she will step closer to him, recognizing in some way his humiliation, and wanting to make him feel better, but he will think she is about to say or do something even worse than she has already done, and he will misinterpret her gesture. When she gets close to him, he will kick her in the stomach—harder than he has ever kicked anyone.

He will regret this before she even begins to cry. She will double over, gasping for breath, and look up at him with dry eyes, and he will know that the hurt he has just inflicted upon her is at least equal to but probably greater than the hurt caused to him by the *y* of her laughter.

He will feel terrible, and he will immediately think back to *x*, the variable that started this whole rotten equation.

Let x equal not the moment just after he tells her about the computer club, but the moment just before it.

Let x be his saying nothing about this club and instead telling her something he's always wanted to say.

Let x be a different gesture altogether. Something honest. Tender.

Let x.

fourteen

i. the things a dirty mouth might be capable of

jodee likes the baseball players, with their tight white pants and their mitts cut from cow cloth, but everybody knows it's safe to like a boy's butt, which is made of out nothing but skin and blood and fat. no boy in the history of the world ever raped a girl with his ass.

while jodee sits in the bleachers and fantasizes about the butts that remind her of marshmallows, and the ones that make her want to bounce a quarter off them, i'm down at the football stadium, watching track practice. when they practice, most of the track guys take off their shirts, and i'm pretty sure jodee has never seen in the flesh a body like the one on that guy who throws the javelin.

jodee can stay up at the baseball field all day and night for all i care. she can touch knees with jenni and giggle every time jordan or sam adjusts his cup. she can say *eww* when the boys sneak a pinch of dip behind the coach's back, and then she can disregard entirely the things a dirty mouth might be capable of.

i'll take that javelin thrower right over there and forget about jodee in the time it takes him to get a good grip on that spear. he looks relaxed right now, casual, his bangs down in his eyes, the javelin and a hot white spot of sun on his muscle-y shoulder, but anybody—probably even jodee—can see that this guy is about to uncoil like a spring.

ii. marks

i'd convinced my parents to let me stay at home for the weekend while they drove to champaign for my sister's graduation. i'd told them i had two papers and a lab report to finish, and did they want me to fail the majority of the classes i was taking in the second half of my first year of high school? they did not.

but then one of ryan's friends—i'm not sure which one, though i'm betting it was sam or jordan—taped a note accompanied by an anatomically impossible drawing to our mailbox asking when was it his turn for a blow job.

mom and dad decide in all of three seconds that i can do my work in the car, and at the hotel.

i spend a few hours on friday afternoon in the backseat of their audi, wearing earbuds and punching the keys on my laptop too hard, and we arrive at katie's apartment at around seven to take her to dinner.

mom calls katie from the parking lot to say we're there, and then my phone buzzes. i'd told ryan that i'd have the house to myself on friday and saturday, and i hadn't told him any different after one of his douche-bag friends—who shouldn't even have known about what had happened to begin with—got all horny and picasso and decided to exhibit his work on our front porch. i figured ryan was just then showing up at the house, full of hope and charged with expectations.

i glance down at the phone and tug an earbud free, trying to decide if i will take ryan's call at all when i see katie's name on the screen.

katie and i are seven years apart. we aren't close. i'm surprised her name is even in my phone.

there is a text message: *come up? tell mom and dad you have to use the restroom or something.*

katie answers the door with one hand pressed to the side of her neck. with her unoccupied hand, she pulls me inside her apartment like she hasn't eaten for a few days and i'm a veggie pizza.

the bruise on katie's neck is terrible—like the mark a seatbelt might leave after an accident.

what happened? i say, and i'm really not sure.

i just want you to help me cover it up, she says.

i lower the toilet seat, tell katie to sit down, and then begin with foundation the color of dried-out apricots. katie's skin is far too pale for it, but it's going to have to do.

when i start in with the powder, katie's roommate comes out of her bedroom and stops in front of the open bathroom door. her eyes are red and raw-looking. her hands, balled up into fists, look heavy as stones at her sides.

she is wide enough that she just about fills the doorway, but she's short, so she's like a gate but with bad hair. she and katie have been roommates for three years, but i've only seen her a few times, and never quite like this. i think her name is megan. she stares at us and sniffles.

i'm standing over my sister, straddling her. i'm cupping her face in one of my hands. she pulls her head back and turns toward the door. *go away,* she says. then she closes her eyes and puts her cheek back inside my palm.

megan runs her forearm beneath her nose to clean up some dripping snot. she points a finger at me like she is about to orate, like she is about to passionately address a throng of zealous millions, but then she retreats. about the time she presses her door closed — she doesn't slam it — i begin to realize the nature of what has just happened.

the drawing that had been left on our mailbox was of two stick figures. the girl stick figure was recognizable as such by the lines that made up her long hair, by her big round eyes, and by the feminine tilt of her head as she knelt on her hands and knees and attempted to swallow a penis that, if it were brought to life in proportion with its stick body, would be capable of impregnating god. whoever drew the picture had also written my name beneath the girl and run an arrow up toward her breast-less chest. Everything about that picture was obvious in a way that this moment between my sister and her roommate isn't.

katie? i say. the powder brush is light as ten feathers, but it hasn't moved in so long it's getting heavy.

katie opens her eyes. she speaks with her cheek still touching my hand.

she wanted me to tell mom and dad about us before graduation, she says. *she wanted me to come out. the hickey is a punishment.*

the bathroom light is fluorescent. it flickers twice as the last seven or eight years of my sister's life become for me less blurry around the edges.

if it were up to me, i would wipe clean the foundation and powder i have already applied and present katie and her scarlet-letter-like hickey to my parents on a platter. if i did these things, i would get to live for a moment in a world that was a little more honest — and i would get to watch my parents seethe.

but i have love for Katie inside me sure as blood. and besides, none of this is really up to me.

ok, i say, readying my brush, holding her head still in my hand. *we're going to fix this up good.*

---

iii. when we were girls

i'm not a lesbian like my sister but i think sometimes about jodee.

i don't think i could ever kiss her with an open mouth, or run my hand up her shirt, but when she passes by me in the hall at school without so much as a glance, when she releases into the air one of those laughs so impure it's like a bad pop song, i wonder what it would be like to do something to her, to touch her in a way that's different from the way we would touch when we were girls. i wonder what it would be like to stare into her stupid face while I did it, saying, *look at me, goddamnit. look. i'm right here.*

Obnubilate

---

verb tr.: to cloud over, obscure, or darken

I.

A week after her mastectomy, my mom's head throbs. She feels every couple of minutes like she is about to puke.

She thinks it's the flu, which has been going around, even though she's only left the house twice for trips to the doctor.

I ask her what she'll do if she has to throw up.

"I can't hear you," she says. "You're breaking up."

I have seen the incision, an eleven-inch gash that runs like a crooked smile from her sternum to some hidden place beneath her armpit. It's pink near the stitches, tender looking.

A couple days ago, when Mom asked me if I wanted to see it, it didn't look like the kind of thing that could endure much retching.

I ask her again what she'll do if she gets sick, and again she tells me I'm breaking up.

It's not the connection. It's the way I hold my phone—pointed toward my left shoulder instead of my mouth—while I pace around the downstairs of my house, from the kitchen to the dining room, to the foyer, then back to the kitchen. Over and over, I walk in this loop and talk into empty air.

I realize this is the problem, but still I keep doing it. I let her think the connection is going bad until she can't stand it anymore and tells me she's hanging up, she'll try me again tomorrow.

II.

My mom finds out when she sees her surgeon two days later that she doesn't have the flu. The doctor says there's a seroma, an infection-filled sack of pus, under her arm, and that this seroma is what is making her sick.

The doctor drains the pus with a syringe, but hours later, my mom's incision is leaking again. The fluid is brownish and odorless, not very thick.

"You wouldn't believe it," my mom says to me, her voice part thrilled, part sickened. "There's so much of it! It's disgusting."

It had seemed impossible that she would have ended up with the flu. She'd been mostly alone for days, ever since she was discharged.

At the hospital, there were signs stuck to the walls every few feet in every corridor, encouraging people to cover their coughs, to wash their hands.

"I've had to change my shirt twice already today," my mom says.

At the bottom of the posters, there was a message: We Are All In This Together.

It seemed so ominous. I wondered, Who is this *we*? What is this *this*?

What my mom tells me reminds me of a dream I had once, in which I woke up and walked from my bed to the bathroom and stared at myself, shirtless, in the mirror over the sink. Right away, my mouth opened, and in the mirror I watched thick greenish mucus stream from my face into the basin. I was a dirty fountain, a broken vessel, and the dream was all the more vivid because in it I had woken up, and so was tricked into thinking everything was real.

I could feel the sludge passing through my neck, entering my mouth.

When I really did wake up, I was coughing, choking, disgusted.

It shows poor judgment, but I tell my mom about this dream, in every last detail I can recall.

"That's horrible," she says. "That sounds really awful."

I can tell by the way she says it that she means it. That she actually cares. That she is reacting so strongly to this thing I have told her about that was only a goddamn dream.

III.

My wife is sitting up next to me in bed, her laptop propped on a pillow set across her legs. There is a TV on in front of us, but I'm talking again to my mom.

She is still leaking infection from the incision on her chest where her breast used to be. "The antibiotics are working, though," she says. "The pus is, like, less brown now."

My wife is close enough she can hear what my mom is saying, and she swivels her laptop in my direction. I can see from the webpage's layout that she's done a Google image search, but the icons are small enough I can't see what they are.

My wife loves Google image search. In the past, she has swiveled her laptop and revealed to me a page filled with micropenises—or baby hummingbirds.

My mom lets me know for the seventh or eighth time just how gross the stuff is that leaks from her body. I lean toward my wife's computer to get a better look.

The images are tough to make out. The first might be a dog or a horse. The second is of some medical equipment. The third looks like a linoleum floor.

I make a face at my wife. I shrug. She whispers, "I did a search for seroma." She points at the picture of the linoleum floor and says, "Look."

My mom says that she wonders some mornings why she bothers even to get dressed. She's soiling one shirt after another, all day long.

Where my wife's finger hovers near the screen, I make out a brown puddle in the shape of some fresh scab, some old continent, on the linoleum, right in front of a refrigerator. Several of the images look like this one, like something that has been spilled.

You can only take a photograph of a seroma, it seems, after the infection has left the body. Until then, you can capture only skin. You could stare at that skin for hours in fact, really searching it, and never have a clue about what might be right there beneath it.

IV.

It took less than a minute for my mom to ask me if I wanted to see her incision after she was released from the hospital. I walked in the back door of her house, and the first words out of her mouth were, "Want to see it?"

I told her I did, though I wasn't sure.

There were two drain tubes inserted in her chest then, slowing filling with wheat-colored fluid.

"Wow," I said.

My mom was smiling, proud. She had unzipped her pink pullover and was holding its front open as if she were peeling back her skin and revealing to me her screaming and throbbing heart.

She is only fifty-five. A speed limit. She has loved video games since I was a kid, and when I was young, she would punish my brother and me by sending us to the TV room, because she wanted to play with the Nintendo in our bedroom.

Her favorite games for a long time were The Legend of Zelda and Metroid. She took her time with Zelda — she kept a notebook, made maps — but she went at Metroid a little more fiercely, wanting to finish it as soon as she began. She kept falling short, though, day after day. Mother Brain kept doing her in. Finally, one day, my brother and I returned home from school, and my mom was ecstatic. She repeated, "I beat Mother Brain! I beat Mother Brain!" over and over.

The look on her face then, it was almost the exact look on her face when she was showing me the new incision on her chest. Only her face was younger then, fuller in the cheeks, with fewer lines and freckles.

She had not yet beaten a thing, of course, sitting there in her pink pullover, holding open her shirt for me. The doctors were still saying chemotherapy. They were saying anti-hormone injections. They were saying the next six months are not going to be fun.

But my mom wasn't thinking about those things right then. She was thinking only of that gash in her chest, how it curved toward her armpit like a terrible and dangerous road. She was proud of it. She was shining with pride.

Tell
Everyone
I Said
Hi

It's the end of October, and Clover and I have put
away our lawn mowers for the winter. We mowed our last round
of yards the other day—well, mostly we mulched fallen leaves.
The weather was perfect: the sky cloudless and blue, the air like
a brisk walk through the woods. My skin hovered on that fine
brink of near-sweating all day and made me forget those heavy-
aired, can't-keep-the-sweat-out-of-your-eyes July and August af-
ternoons we mowed through. All of Rosewater smelled good, and
I swear I could feel each breath work inside my lungs.

We saved your great aunt Margarite's yard for last. She came
outside when we were through and told me she'd be needing

someone to shovel snow soon. "Let me know if *you* need anything until then," she said.

I told her I would.

You are the thing Margarite and I never talk about, the thing we take awkward little baby steps around, though I'm sure you're right there in both our minds.

She paid me and smiled that perfect set of false teeth at me, and there was something sweet and sorrowful in her smile, which made me think of you again, and how it most likely hurts her just as bad as it does me to feel like we aren't supposed to mention you.

"I know about Lizzie," I said, even though you probably already told her I called, and then Margarite said, "Oh, Lonnie," and hugged me.

It felt good to hug Aunt Margarite again. She's so soft in your arms, but strong, and that big, blond beehive hairdo of hers clung to the side of my face when our heads almost touched. She smelled like White Rain hairspray and beer.

Once Margarite headed inside, Clover and I loaded our mowers into the back of the truck—it still has your name next to mine on the doors—and took off for home. The clocks are an hour behind now here, and the sky was going dark a little sooner than it seemed it should.

I know you don't set your clocks back. You're on the other side of that invisible line they've drawn in Indiana, which means it stays lighter there a little longer each evening.

I get sentimental over the silliest things anymore. Goddamn light. I can't stand it sometimes.

I can't say exactly why I called.

I keep trying to imagine you pregnant. I get your face, I get your belly, a little blown up, but I can't connect the two. I can't make it real.

I bet your dad is ecstatic. Sometimes I miss old Winslow as much as anything. I remember walking into his house for the first time and Lucky One putting his one front paw up on my chest, over my heart.

I always thought it was perfect for him to own a three-legged dog, the same way he roots for the Cubs and the Seattle Seahawks. It's no wonder he always liked me so much.

———————

The day we finished at Margarite's, Clover was driving the truck, and I had my arm hanging out the open window. We were getting ready for a little end-of-the-mowing-season celebration, Clover and me. It wasn't going to be anything special, really—another night at Tootie's—but we were going to pretend it was special. We were going to have a reason for being out.

The air outside still felt warm, the truck smelled like gasoline, and the grass and leaves stuck to our jeans. I should've been feeling pretty good. But dusk was all around us, and I kept thinking about how it gets darker out in Indiana sooner than it does in Illinois, even if it is later in the evening. And then I imagined standing outside the house you and Ted bought. I imagined that big picture window you told me about, and I saw myself standing outside that window, in the street, seeing the two of you through the curtains, silhouetted in this golden light.

The two of you weren't doing anything special. You were sitting on the couch, facing one another. I could see a blue smear of light, the TV, in the corner of the room, but I couldn't make out what program was on. You were talking, moving your hands in the air like you do. I kept trying to but couldn't hear a word you said.

Clover and I were going home, and my God it's stupid but I was sitting there wishing I could pull the sun up from the horizon, just jerk that son of a bitch up, to keep it light outside a little bit longer. So I wouldn't have to stand out in the dark and see Ted and you in that golden light through the window.

———————

I won't call you again.

What I didn't like about calling was how I ended the conversation. Clover was in the other room with one of his college girls, and what I wanted more than anything was to keep talking to you, to never stop. But I could tell you were sleepy, and I knew your boyfriend—fiancé, I mean (do you use that word? does he?)—was waiting for you to return to bed so he could wrap his arm around that belly I can't even truly picture. So he could smell that peach-shampoo smell at the nape of your neck.

I wish I could hate this guy Ted. I do. I really hope he doesn't call you his fiancée.

What happened at the end of our call was I started getting anxious. I felt like I hadn't said anything. It was just so good to hear you happy, and everything you'd said started to fill up my head so all I wanted was for you to keep filling it up, to fill it completely.

And then you were gently letting me know you were ready to go back to bed. Your voice was full of sweetness and maybe a little sorrow too, like Aunt Margarite's smile the other day, and I could barely take it. Your voice—it was more than just sweetness and sorrow. It sounded like you pitied me, like I was some kid or pet you felt sorry for. I started hating you then, you and Ted, and that's when I ended up muttering that I wanted you to tell everyone I said hi.

After we hung up I didn't even know what it meant: Tell everyone I said hi. I said it over and over again, the phone still in my hand. It seemed like the absolute stupidest thing in the world a person could say.

———   ———

You know, I can't get drunk anymore. I drink the same as always, but I can't get the alcohol to take the way it used to. It's not so bad really. I still catch an okay buzz, only it won't go from a hey-this-night-isn't-going-to-be-so-bad-after-all drunk to a piss-on-the-living-room-floor-in-the-middle-of-the-night drunk. I can't even remember the last time I forgot what time I fell asleep.

Clover thinks there's something wrong with me. I don't tell him much, but he's starting to figure things out on his own. He says I'm about as difficult to read as a billboard.

Clover still wears an eyepatch over his left eye to bed because of how that eye blurs when he's drunk. He still sleeps on the sofa. He's rigged the VCR now so it plays *Star Wars* all night long, over and over, like a CD set to repeat.

Something else that's new: Clover's achieved a reputation with the college girls. He's slept with a number of them, sort of. He never finishes. Can you imagine? Never. He says he hasn't successfully slept with a woman in more than a year. It's the effects of liquor, no doubt, but the girls think he's some kind of superhero.

I've been trying to figure out why I can't get drunk, and I think it's my liver. I think all those years I drank only served to make my liver stronger, the way boxers jump rope to condition their lungs, and now my liver can cleanse my body of alcohol quicker than most people's can. I know that sounds backward, but it's the best explanation I've come up with.

Clover brings one particular girl home all the time now. Her name's Della. She's majoring in elementary education and keeps trying to talk Clover into going back to school to be a gym teacher. Della's a cutie. She has these tattoos, they're on her feet. Clover lets her stay over sometimes. He wears the eyepatch and watches *Star Wars* with her right there on the couch with him.

The tattoos on Della's feet are tiny red and yellow stars, and she wears shoes that make it so they're always visible. When Della and Clover go to bed at night, they start off sleeping at opposite ends of the couch. She puts her bare, tattooed feet up on his chest, and he looks at them with his uncovered eye.

He's hoping she'll be the woman he finally has some success sleeping with, but he's worried about what may happen once he does.

He likes the idea of going back to school and becoming a gym teacher. He likes that she thinks his eyepatch is cute.

I am trying to hope for nothing but good things for both of them.

I don't know why I never thought you'd move away once you graduated. When I bought the truck and made my mowing gigs an official business—with your name in the title and painted on the doors—I'd planned on you sticking around. Not that a little paint job was my way of showing I was committed to you. I know I had five years to ask you to marry me.

Looking back on our last few months together, it seems Winslow knew things were about to change. There was one day we were together out in his yard with Lucky One. We had the radio tuned to a Cubs game, and your dad was sitting in that chair next to his garage, at the wooden table where he keeps the radio. The Cubs were getting pounded, and Ron Santo sounded hurt as hell each time the other team scored a run.

I was tossing around a tennis ball for the dog to fetch, and you were at the library, studying. It was mid-April, a few weeks before your last set of finals. I was wearing jeans and no shirt, and I was really getting into watching Lucky hop after the tennis ball each time I threw it.

I gave the ball a good toss—all the way to the neighbor's yard—and chuckled a little as the dog bolted after it. I swear he's the fastest living thing on three legs. I turned to Winslow, wanting to say as much, but he was all slumped over, his elbows on his knees. He looked like he might cry.

"What gives, Win?" I said. "You of all people should know better than to let the Cubs' losing get you down."

I know you don't like hearing about your mom, but I want to tell you about this. Here's what Winslow said that day: "You know I don't even know where Ginny lives anymore."

Lucky dropped the slobbery ball at my feet. I picked it up and accidentally wiped it off on my bare chest, trying to figure out what to say back.

"She used to say I needed to pay more attention to the small things," he said.

Lucky sat in front of me, panting, balanced as a tripod.

"What are 'the small things'?" he said. He held his hands in front of him like he expected something to drop into them. "Maybe if I'd made dinner for her once in a while," he said.

I tossed the ball into the neighbor's yard again, but Lucky didn't take out after it. Your dad was headed for the house, and Lucky followed him, hopping in this defeated way up the back steps.

The radio was still playing, and the Cubs, well, they were getting killed. I hurried home, trying to think of some small thing I could do that might make you happy.

That was the same night you fell asleep at the library and didn't get home until midnight. The night of our last big fight.

I was drunk by the time you got home. And angry. You walked

in all frazzled, your hair matted on one side, a tired smile on your face. "What's that smell?" you said. "Have you been cooking?"

I started toward the kitchen for another beer, and you kept sniffing the air. "It smells great in here," you said. You looked like a happy sleepwalker, or someone just waking up from a good dream.

And that's when I said something like, "I don't smell a god-damned thing," and I got the ball rolling on that fight I'd spent the last few hours just dying to have.

Sometimes when Clover is drunk and doesn't bring a girl home and we're sitting in the living room having a final beer or two, he'll turn to me and say he wishes he had what I have. He's talking about you when he says it. He says it like he thinks we're still together. It's times like those I wish hard I could still get drunk, so I could trick myself into thinking I have what I had.

About your name still being written on the truck's door: I wasn't lying—it is—but there's no one but you or me who could read it. There was this incident a while back that involved me not being drunk—despite my best efforts, I mean, I was really trying—and the forked end of a tire iron.

I was so happy when you decided to go to college. I used to think of it as something you were doing for both of us, that you were preparing us for a better life.

It wasn't until you started to take more hours, so you could graduate in three years instead of four, that I began to see school as something you were doing more for you than us. I was still proud of you, though. I still liked looking at your grade reports on the refrigerator door. I still liked calling you my college girl.

You remember that game the two of us used to play when we would go to Tootie's? We'd get dressed up and drive there together. You'd go inside, take a seat at the bar, and I'd wait a few minutes before going in and then sit somewhere across from you. We made eyes for a while. You tossed your hair around, acted bored. I played shy and nervously asked Mike to put another of whatever you were having on my tab.

We weren't fooling anyone, of course, except maybe a few of the college kids. But there was always a moment, right before you got up and came to take a seat by me, to thank me for the drink, when I was amazed we were together.

I'd watch you tuck a few strands of hair behind your ear and make your eyes all big, and I would forget you were mine. I would want you more than anything, but I'd think you were unattainable, out of my league, and I'd start to panic, thinking you wouldn't come over to me after all.

You did, of course. Every time. And every time it felt like someone was massaging my stomach from the inside out, with long, soft fingers.

_____

It's probably silly, but I wonder sometimes about that day your dad brought up your mom. I wonder exactly what he saw coming—you getting that job in Kokomo and moving away from him or you moving away from me. I imagine he was thinking both things, but I wonder which one it was had him about to cry.

It kills me to think the guy who was once my greatest cheerleader now roots for some guy named Ted. Sometimes I think I could strangle him, this guy Ted I've never even met.

_____

On the night we were celebrating the end of our employment, Clover told me Della was setting me up with one of her friends, a girl named Jaime. He didn't say so until we were in the truck on our way to Tootie's.

"Why don't you just drop me off at Second Street then," I said. You remember that place, the one with HOME OF THE POOR AND UNKNOWN written on their matchbooks?

"Don't say that," Clover said. "You giving up on me?"

"Oh, I still have hope," I said. "I am filled up with it."

Clover laughed until we pulled into the parking lot.

Inside, we ordered beers and sat at the bar. The smoky air was like gauze — I could feel it wrapping me up, salving me.

Della came over, giving us a good look at those little constellations on her feet. "No pressure, Lonnie," she told me. "We'll play a game of darts or something."

The four of us played a game, guys against girls, and the girls kept it pretty close.

Jaime was cute. She had her hair done in these little braids and pulled back off her forehead. The hair seemed strange, but Jamie had a nice forehead — smooth and flat and tanned — and bright blue eyes. She's studying business, same as you did. When the game was over Della and Clover went out to the dance floor and left Jaime and me sitting at the table near the dartboards. We talked for a bit, and then she got up, put one hand on my shoulder, and said, "I'm going to go find someone to dance with."

That really made me laugh.

I bellied up to the bar and ordered another beer, thinking this was a pretty okay night after all. Jaime'd found herself a college boy, and she and the boy and Della and Clover were all out there dancing. The music was loud, the place was filling up, and then this pregnant woman walked in and took a seat two stools down from me.

A part of me wanted to lay into her for being at the bar. I mean, this woman had a child growing inside her. She didn't look that far along, maybe four or five months, about the same as you. Her belly pooched out some and looked firm, taut.

She ordered a glass of milk and made herself comfortable on the stool. I wasn't necessarily thinking about you, but I was thinking about that game we used to play. I started keeping an eye on the door, expecting this woman's husband to come through.

She looked like she might be waiting for some man to come walking through the door. She wore her makeup thick, and her hair was fixed like it was done by a professional — all big and airy and too perfect. Mike served her the milk in a Tom Collins glass with a long green straw standing up out of it, and the woman took little baby sips from the straw, marking it with a ring of red from her lipstick.

I waited a few minutes more, but no husband or boyfriend

showed up, and then I started to think maybe I *should* tell this woman what I thought about her being pregnant and coming to a bar. I figured one more minute and she's going to get a blue cigarette case out of her purse and light one up.

I grabbed my beer and coaster and hopped over a seat. "Howdy," I said. "I'm Lonnie."

I don't know why I was so angry. I think maybe I did imagine for a second she was you and that we were still together the way Clover sometimes thinks we are. And for some reason I could see you being pregnant and in a bar if you were still with me, and I hated the whole idea of us ever being together.

The pregnant woman wrapped her bright red lips around her straw and took a little sip. "I'm Lucinda," she said. She put the drink down and smiled at me like I was some kind of angel, like I was just what she'd ordered, and, well, that kind of pushed me over the edge.

I hollered at Mike, "Two shots of bourbon, to the rims."

Mike set the two shots on the bar, and Lucinda put a hand to the side of her head, fluffing up that professional-style hairdo of hers, all coy and flirty.

"Well, come on, Lucy," I said. "Belly up. Shot's waitin'."

Her hand dropped, and I noticed her fingernails. Their tips were painted white in neat little lines. Probably had them fixed at the same time as her hair.

I held the shot up in the air for her, and her face closed up like a fist. Then she tried a smile that kind of died before it ever came alive. She said, "I—I couldn't." Her left hand made a small circle on her belly.

I shoved the shot toward her with the kind of force I'd put on a man, and she raised a hand to block it. Most of the bourbon splashed in an arc and then settled in the pouffy hair on the side of her head, ruining it.

She made a face, and right away I felt very small. I reached behind the bar for some napkins, frantic, with both hands. Mike grabbed one of my arms. He said, "Goddamn, Lonnie," and in a few seconds he'd escorted me out the door, away from the pregnant woman who was not you. I didn't even have it in me to put up a fight.

Old Winslow doesn't know where your mom is. I have at least that much, but sometimes I think ignorance would be a little bliss.

Other times, I wonder what would've happened that night I made dinner for you and you didn't come home until midnight, if I hadn't gotten drunk and taken everything—the cloth napkins, the candles, the chicken enchiladas—and set fire to them in the alley. Would things be any different if we'd eaten cold Mexican food by candlelight at midnight?

I'm having that problem now, like the one I had when I called. I'm feeling anxious, and I kind of want to just say, "Tell everyone I said 'Hi.'" Something stupid and meaningless.

I'll tell you this instead: I gave Clover my recipe for chicken enchiladas, and he's out in the kitchen right now preparing them for Della.

It was mostly browned garlic you smelled that night, when you kept sniffing the air, wondering if I'd cooked. I'd browned garlic for the chicken.

Right now the whole apartment smells like browned garlic.

I keep breathing it in. I can't get enough.

Glass

The house's windows were old, warped—nothing looked right through them.

He was curious enough to look it up on the Internet at the library, and he learned that the wavy outside he and his girlfriend saw through the windows was caused not by the flow of glass over time—by years of a gradual, continuous, invisible trickle—but by the glass's imperfections. A perfectly flat pane of glass, he found out, wasn't invented all that long ago.

She worked six shifts a week at the bookstore and complained about how much her feet hurt. "What twenty-one-year-old," she said, "complains of sore feet? This is killing me."

He worked with homeless men — took down their personal histories, directed them toward community resources.

When their schedules didn't keep them apart during the week, he told her he thought he was becoming addicted to sad, that some days he couldn't get enough of it. "It has to be wrong," he said. "I shouldn't like this so much."

On Saturday nights, they would buy a big bottle of wine and a twelve-pack of Coors. They'd check out a movie from the library and watch maybe half of it, and then they'd walk to the porn shop a few blocks away. They'd rent a movie, buy a toy.

On the way back, they'd stop in the park between the porn shop and the house with the old windows, and they would lie down in the grass. It would be dark save a distant streetlight or two, and they would feel the wind on the sides of their faces as they kissed. They would rustle leaves.

He would ask her to let him fuck her there in the park, and she'd say no, she couldn't. He'd plead a little, beg, and then they'd head home, drink more, take the stairs up to bed.

Sometimes, he only wanted to use the new toy on her. "Just lie there," he would say. "Pretend your hands are tied to the bed frame. Pretend you can't move them."

Other times she would say, "It's my turn," and she'd grab one of the toys from the dresser. "But first," she would say, searching along the floor for a pair of nylons, pulling them taut in her fists, "give me your hands."

How many mornings did they come downstairs in that house — hungover, wiping the sleep from their eyes, forgetting they'd walked away from the park the night before with their pants still unbuttoned, forgetting they'd ever even been there?

How many mornings did they look through the downstairs windows — the world outside runny, imperfect — expecting to see something different, only to find a tree or two, some leaves, the neighbor walking his dog?

American
Bulldog

The night before, her socks leached rainwater from the carpet in the basement. The dehumidifier was running. The sump pump still churned. Everything important—her sewing machine table, the desk with her art supplies—was up on blocks from the previous fall, and Anna figured it might as well all stay that way, at least for now: It had rained for four straight days, and who knew how much water was going to seep through the foundation walls before it stopped.

In bed, after she changed her socks and was snuggled and warm under the covers, Anna hoped she would dream of floods—the biblical kind, of arks and utter devastation. But she woke up a little before five to the sound of rain against her bedroom window and with no memory of the previous night's dreams at all. Leslie the dog was at attention outside her bedroom door when she opened it.

"Come on, then," Anna said, and Leslie followed her to the three-season room, where Anna let him out into the dark, wet backyard.

She put on a pot of coffee, and before she went to retrieve Leslie, she lit the basement stairs and began walking down them to see what kind of damage may have been done overnight.

Halfway down to the turn in the stairs, Anna heard water sloshing. She heard a muffled buzzing sound that may have been the dehumidifier but sounded like it was coming from a long way off. When she reached the turn, Anna saw that at least three but maybe four or five steps were submerged in water. Her basement, dimly lit, looked like the edge of a lake.

The water was still, but Anna could feel a coolness coming off it. She rubbed her hands over her forearms and squinted her eyes. A clear plastic tub filled with wrapping paper floated past the front of the stairs and knocked against the wood-paneled wall.

There were things in the basement she wanted to get out of there before they were ruined—a quilt she was sewing for one of her adult grandchildren, a needle-point project she'd been working on for months—but she'd heard about people being electrocuted in situations just like this. Those people took one step into the water and never breathed another breath. Who knew how long it took somebody to find them, drifting facedown among the debris of their basements, bloated with floodwater.

Anna ascended the stairs and realized she was hiking up her nightgown with one hand, as if it were in danger of becoming wet.

When she reached the three-season room, she saw Leslie standing at the screen door, staring at her, waiting to be let inside. Anna opened the door and grabbed the towel she kept on the patio table nearby.

"Come here, you," she said, and the dog stood at her feet. Anna draped the towel over his sides and patted him down. Leslie shook himself once, and again, pelting Anna with sprinkles. Anna patted him a little harder than she needed to. She hated this little ritual. She hated being in such close contact with the dog.

She told Leslie to sit, and then she picked up each of his front paws so she could dry them off. When she was done, the dog stood, and Anna dried each of his back paws, too. "Get going," Anna said, and made a motion with her hand. The dog trotted off, and while Anna wiped flecks of mud and leaves off her hands onto the towel, she heard Leslie's nails clacking on the kitchen linoleum. She thought about the body of water in her basement—about the books down there whose pages were becoming swollen, about the way water warps wood. The flooding wasn't as bad around here as it was in places like Gulfport, where the rainwater had pushed the Mississippi beyond its banks and right into town. The whole place had been evacuated. The farmers near there were looking out on land their families had owned for over a hundred years and seeing nothing but river. Still, Anna was unnerved.

The coffee had finished brewing, and she poured herself a cup, then stared at the open door that led down to the basement. She brought her mug to her nose, hoping to lose herself for a moment in its aroma and warmth, but she could hear water through the doorway. She imagined more tubs floating by the stairs in the dim light, tiny aimless ships on a vast sea.

And then she thought of her projects again—the things that needed saving.

Leslie came into the kitchen and took his usual seat in front of the refrigerator door. The linoleum was heated, and the dog settled onto his belly and let his chin rest on the floor, as if there weren't anything at all wrong in the world.

Anna set her coffee cup down on the counter and walked over to Leslie. His eyes were closed, and already he was drooling a small puddle of spittle onto the linoleum.

"Hey, you," she said, nudging the dog with her foot. "Meat-head. Wake up."

The dog looked up and tipped his head to the side, his tongue hanging stupidly out of his mouth.

Anna and her husband, Leslie, had spent forty-one years of marriage utterly pet-less, and had raised two kids who begged them on a regular basis for an animal of some kind they could take care of.

The kids at first wanted a dog, of course. But after Leslie said no way, after he complained about how dogs just tear up the house and then ask you to take them for a walk, the kids moved on to asking for other animals over the years. Cats, birds, even fish, which were almost no fun at all. Leslie had said that it was a slippery slope, that he didn't want anything with a beating heart inside his house except for his wife and the children she had birthed.

Anna had felt a little sorry for the kids. She'd watched Vicky, now married and living in Chicago and with grown kids of her own, check out and read from cover to cover each book on dogs shelved at the Galesburg Public Library. Vicky knew every breed's origins, and how well it could see and smell and hear. She knew what its tongue looked like. The girl's devotion, the depth of her knowledge, broke Anna's heart.

But Leslie would not give in, even after Michael for a while refused to watch any television show that did not feature in some way an animal. Even after the boy wallpapered his bedroom with pencil drawings of schnauzers and terriers he'd traced from Vicky's library books.

The kids' efforts at securing a cat or a parakeet or a goldfish were actually a little weak, Anna thought. All they ever really wanted was a dog.

But Leslie wouldn't have it.

That is, until right after he retired, when he returned from one of his drives to God-knows-where with a fully grown American bulldog leashed to his arm.

"What should we name him?" he asked Anna in the three-season room.

The back of Anna's hand drifted to her forehead. "Oh, Leslie," she said, not wanting the dog to step foot inside her house. It had beady eyes and one black ear. Its tongue was a wide pink stripe.

"Yes," Leslie said. "Ha! We'll call him Leslie."

Anna turned back toward the house. "You can call him whatever you want," she said.

And Leslie did call him, often. He called him into Anna and Leslie's bed at night, where the dog slept right on top of Anna's comforter, draped over Leslie's legs. He called him out to the car, and the two of them disappeared together for hours. When Anna and Leslie drove to church on Sunday mornings, the car smelled as if the dog were hiding somewhere in the backseat.

Everything Anna touched seemed to smell like bulldog. It was the smell, Anna thought, of her husband's retirement, and it infuriated her.

Anna had retired several years before Leslie, and while she had enjoyed her time at home alone—mildly redecorating the place and taking up sewing and needlepoint—she had been excited about Leslie's retirement. About the things they might do together, like going for walks or playing tennis. And then no sooner than he had stopped working for Burlington Northern, her husband had brought another beating heart into their house. Another thing to put a little distance between his wife and him now that they could be alone together.

And then, just months after he had brought the dog home—months of agony for Anna, who couldn't sleep right with the dog on the bed the way he always was, and who couldn't buy enough air freshener to cover up the dog's stink—Leslie her husband died of a heart attack after dinner one night as he sat in his recliner with Leslie the dog on his lap, one hand on the back of the dog's head, right between his differently colored ears.

———

Anna walked toward the basement door now and patted herself on the hip. She smiled at the dog. "Come on, boy," she said, realizing as she patted herself on the hip again that she was performing a kind of imitation of her dead husband. How many times those past few months he was alive had she seen him walk past her and say nothing and then start talking to the dog and patting himself on the hip or leg or lap?

Leslie trotted over to her, panting, spritzing the floor with drool.

"We're going down to the basement, doggie," Anna said. She hiked up her nightgown with one hand and began descending the stairs with a ball of fabric in her fist. Leslie followed tentatively behind.

At the turn in the stairs, Anna waited on Leslie, who froze with his hind legs still on the previous step when he saw the water. Anna wondered if the dog could sense some electrical current. If he could smell danger.

In the weeks that followed her husband's death, Anna had felt like she couldn't even grieve properly. Leslie the dog always wanted to be put outside. He was always wandering around the house, whimpering, looking for his true owner. More than once Anna caught the dog in the backyard staring longingly at Leslie's car in the driveway.

When Anna couldn't even walk past the dog anymore without catching his scent and then thinking unkind things, unholy things, about her dead husband, she considered trying to pawn the dog off on Vicky or Michael, or on one of her grown grandchildren. But not one of them even thought to bring it up. When they did mention the dog, they had the nerve to say something about how lucky she was to have him around to keep her company. The idiots.

For a few months, Anna drove by the Knox County Humane Society with her window rolled down, imagining Leslie as one of the barking dogs inside, caged and far away from her. She drove by a couple of the city's parks and imagined taking Leslie to one of them and removing his collar, letting him run until he dropped while she drove away.

But Anna never carried out any of these plans.

It had been six months now of just her and the dog, and she loved him no more than she had before. She wanted him around even less.

"Just a little farther," Anna said, taking another step down. The dog looked at her as if he were uncertain, but it was clear to Anna that he was going to follow her, however reluctantly, if only, perhaps, because this was the first time he had ever heard her use a kind voice with him.

Anna pitied the dog for a moment for his stupid dependence on her attention. For his blind obedience.

She wondered if maybe she would have felt differently about the dog if she'd known him as a puppy. If Leslie hadn't acquired the dog when it was already an adult. It was hard for Anna to imagine hating a puppy, under any circumstances. If I'd known the dog as a puppy, she thought, I probably wouldn't do what I'm about to do.

Anna took another step down, and then another, until the water was just a few inches below her feet. Lit by the bulb over the stairs, the water shone a dull shade of green. Anna was certain now that she heard the dehumidifier running. The thing had to be submerged, but it was still buzzing out there in the dark, doing its best to take away the moisture that was trying to drown it.

She turned, and the dog was still back on the landing, staring at her. Anna patted her hip again. "Come here," she said. "It's OK."

The dog walked down the steps until he was just behind Anna, then positioned himself so that he was sitting on his haunches with his front paws out to the side. Still, he seems to want to please me, Anna thought.

When she had first begun to descend the stairs, Anna had imagined that she was going to have to pick the dog up, but she remembered now that dogs like to swim. Dogs were always doing whatever they could to jump into some body of water.

Anna scooted over on the stair to give the dog clearance.

"OK, buddy," she said, her voice high and light. "Jump."

She waved her arm over the water beneath her, but the dog only stared at her hand, as if it might finally be offering him some kind of treat.

Anna brought her hand back to her chest. She bent her knees and bounced, waving her arm again. "Jump," she said.

The dog remained upright on the stairs, balanced on his long front legs.

Anna felt stupid doing it, but she placed her hands over her head, as if she were a diver. "Like this," she said, flexing her knees and leaning out a little over the water.

The dog took one more step down the stairs. He came to her.

It was as if he were telling her that he would comply, but that he wasn't going to jump into the water of his own accord. She was going to have to pick him up.

"OK, Leslie," she said. She hiked up her nightgown, and maneuvered into a firm position on the stairs, her back to the wall.

When she bent down to pick up the dog, he stretched out his head toward her hand. He wanted her to pet him.

"All right," Anna said. "All right." She scratched between the dog's ears, and under the dog's chin, and he pressed his face into her hand—hard, lovingly.

Well, dog, she thought. This isn't so bad. Maybe it wouldn't be so terrible if this were the beginning and not the end of our life together.

A quick burst of cool air hit her, and Anna stopped petting Leslie and braced herself against the wall.

The sun was just coming up now, and the basement was lighter than it had been. The things drifting in the water were taking on shape, becoming more defined.

"It's now or never," Anna said.

The dog seemed to stretch his neck out toward her as if asking for one more touch from her hand, but Anna bent and scooped her arms under him. He yielded himself to her, was willing to let her pick him up, but still he was heavy. Anna had to set him back down.

She got behind him and again lifted him. He was between her legs now, suspended in the air, and Anna began to rock him, to get some momentum.

She counted, *One*, and wasn't sure she would be able to maintain her hold on the dog until *Three*.

On *Two*, her arms ached. She thought for a moment about whether, if the dog were electrocuted, there would be a sound. Or a smell. She wondered whom she would have to call to wade out into the water and remove the dog from it. Her arms began to give slightly, but by *Three* she had gained enough momentum, and she let the dog go.

The splash he made broke what seemed to be an immaculate stillness. Water splashed onto Anna's socks and gown, and she shivered. She held her arms to her body and rubbed them.

A moment later, Anna realized that she wasn't looking at the dog in the water. After he landed, she had turned and was looking back up the stairs, afraid to see what might have happened.

She listened hard — and for what? The sound of Leslie paddling his front paws in the water, scrabbling for the stairs? A sound like bacon in a hot skillet? She hoped she wouldn't hear anything like that. The thought alone made her sick to her stomach. She gripped her middle with both arms and burped up hot, acidy air.

Anna realized she didn't hear anything at all except for the dehumidifier buzzing, and she gasped. "God damn it," she breathed.

She turned around on the stair, expecting to find Leslie's dead dog body floating there in the water, drifting toward the plastic tub filled with Christmas paper. She was shielding her eyes with one hand, imagining not the dog but the wrapping paper. The wreaths of green holly against a red background. The plain silver, shimmering.

She thought about the first Christmas she'd spent without her husband, just a few months ago, and she realized she wanted nothing more right then than for the dog to be alive.

Anna brought her hand away from her eyes, and there was Leslie. He paddled silently in the water and stared up at her with a look on his face that made Anna think he was waiting for her to tell him what to do next. His dark ear was folded over on top of his head.

"Good boy," Anna said. "Good boy." She clapped her hands and patted her thighs. She couldn't believe how happy she felt. Her giddiness made her feel silly, or simple. But she patted her thighs again and again called out to the dog.

He began to reach for the stairs with his paws, paddling like mad, and Anna decided she couldn't wait for him any longer. She descended the two steps between her and the water.

A chill began in her toes and shot up into her legs, and Anna continued her descent. She walked down into the water until it reached her waist and Leslie put his paws up on her shoulders. His face was right there before her own, and she realized she was still moving forward. Clumsy and cold and wanting to hold the dog to her until he submerged her completely. Until he pushed her down into the freezing water and she held her breath there for a while, keeping her eyes open. She wanted to hold her breath under the icy water until her lungs burned, until she was good and ready to come screaming back to the water's surface, gasping for breath.

Adaptations

Until Karen, he'd never met an adult who was afraid of the water, who didn't know how to swim.

This was just Kentucky—no ocean for miles—but still. Not long after he and his parents moved to Bardstown, into the big house with the big in-ground pool in the backyard, they seemed to have a party every weekend, and there were always people swimming. People diving crooked and awkward from the board in the deep end, splashing. People putting on a pair of goggles and frogging along the bottom, snatching up plastic rings they'd thrown and watched sink just seconds before. People coupling off when it was dark and the pool was lit green and ethereal by its underwater lights to just kind of drift, running their hands over one another's sheened shoulders and necks, while everything beneath the water moved blind and unknowable.

Most of these people were professors like his parents. They listened to NPR while they drove around town in their Subarus, and didn't look so hot in beachwear.

Karen, though, so feared the water she refused even to wear a suit. She took the deck chair in the corner and sat with her back to the fence, wearing a sundress with a conservative neckline and a pair of wedge sandals she would dangle from her pale feet in this sexy way that made you forget she was a biology professor. Looking out on the scene from his bedroom window, he could tell in two blinks that one of these people was not like the others.

When he wandered outside, though, to refill the bowls that held chips or salsa or guacamole, or to freshen some of the guests' drinks—when he saw her up close—she no longer looked as if she'd escaped the set of some French film, shot in black-and-white, with German subtitles. Her left eye listed toward her nose. There was a delicate-looking rash—quarter-size pink splotches—climbing from her collarbone toward her ear. Her hair had been brushed but looked unhealthy. Wispy. As if it might at any moment unlodge from her skull, follicle by follicle.

None of his parents' new friends had kids at the high school, and he hadn't yet talked to a person his age for the past three months, but he was mostly okay with that. For a long time, since way before they'd moved, he had felt bereft without having ever lost a thing.

Which wasn't the case for Karen. She was in her early thirties and already had been widowed, had buried a child. Still, she got dressed up most Saturdays and came to these parties. Still, she sat in that deck chair and looked out over the pool like it was the French Riviera.

Once, during a party late that summer, he stayed in his room all afternoon and into the night with the window open and his eyes closed, just listening. Every half hour or so he would roll over on his bed and speak into a digital voice recorder a thing or two about what he was hearing: *Some bird calls make me want to buy a BB gun. Is that poet outside singing along with the music or being wounded? If you listen long enough to nothing, it makes a sound—it's like you can hear the trees growing, getting older.*

He realized once it was full dark that he hadn't heard Karen say anything for quite a while. He worried she'd left, and right away went to the window to get a look at all he'd been listening to. Karen was there, and so was everyone else, and it was like he'd never seen any of them before in his life. It was like the not-looking for so long had altered everything he saw.

He went to the kitchen and grabbed a fresh pitcher of sangria out of the fridge and carried it outside. Everybody but Karen was in the pool. There were three couples, including his parents, and the women were all on the men's shoulders, about to begin a game of chicken.

Right about the time he set the pitcher down on the outside bar next to the empty, somebody—probably his dad—blew a whistle. He looked first at Karen, who was leaning forward now, her arms resting on her knees, her fingers laced, smiling in the direction of her colleagues, and then at the pool, which was chaos.

Ethel Hale was a little big. She taught chemistry and wore a pink swimsuit with one of those butt ruffles. Two of her husband Tom could fit inside one of those swimsuits, and Tom had Ethel up on his shoulders, the folds of her butt-cover swamping his back. With every step Tom took, he seemed to clamp down on his wife's thighs harder, hoping to hold her in place. Ethel called out, "Slow *down!*" and waved her arms in the air in little circles like she was exercising, looking for balance.

They went down fast together in a jumble of limbs before they even reached the other couples.

Karen laughed from deep in her throat, in a kind way. In the pool, his parents were squaring off against the Albrights. Shane was the poet. Susan taught Psych. They were around his parents' age—mid-forties—and were in pretty good shape. They ate organic, ran half-marathons, and loved to drink. Susan's forearms were rippled with muscle, and she reached out for his mom, growling.

He began walking toward Karen. He knew already that she never swam, that she never so much as dipped a toe in the pool, but he was thoroughly imagining what it would be like to try to walk around with water up to his waist and her on his shoulders. His hands on her thighs, or his arms braced around her calves. He was only sixteen, but he didn't think it would be so hard to keep her up in the air.

His mother yelped and told his father to circle right. Karen crossed one leg over the other and looked up at him.

He hadn't said anything to anyone in hours, and he wondered if his voice would work when he finally tried to speak. He cleared his throat.

He wanted to ask Karen if she had nightmares about the water—so that he might begin to understand her fear. He wanted to ask her if her house smelled different now that her husband and child were no longer in it. He wanted to ask her why she came to these parties to begin with. He couldn't imagine what this group of people had to offer her.

He decided to begin by saying something about the sangria. Her glass was still full, and he was going to ask her if it tasted all right.

His parents and the Albrights splashed and shrieked. Karen dangled her shoe so that it nearly fell and then snapped it back into place with a thwack.

He focused on her eye—the one that drifted sometimes toward her nose in a way that was remarkably and undeniably cute—and took one final breath. Before he could speak, though, she held up a hand and started talking about caterpillars. She'd been studying them, and there was something about them that she wanted him to know. She didn't look at him while she talked—she kept her eyes on the pool—and so he turned away from her, too, and watched the chicken match while he listened.

"The thing is," Karen said, "these caterpillars are basically defenseless. For millions of years, they've had no way of fighting back, of keeping this or that bird from snatching them up and swallowing them whole."

His mother gave his father more instructions—crouch low, stand up tall, move left—and Susan Albright did the same thing. The men mostly laughed and tried to keep their balance, but the women had no humor in their faces. Tom and Ethel Hale had stopped watching the fight and were kissing without tongue near the deep end.

"So how have they survived?" Karen asked. "What is it that has happened over all these years to keep them alive? Why are there still butterflies?"

He got the idea from the dreamy way she was asking the questions that she wasn't expecting him to answer, that she was going to keep talking. He kept his eyes on the pool, though they had kind of defocused.

"They've adapted," Karen said. "Up close, a lot of caterpillars have the face of a snake. They have odd- and dangerous-looking little horns. They have tail whips, false eyespots."

He couldn't remember ever looking at a caterpillar up close. He tried to imagine what all these things would look like but couldn't. All he could imagine was the person right there beside him. The one he wasn't looking at but whom he knew was wearing a sundress and had one leg crossed prettily over the other. The one who was looking out at the pool just like he was. He heard more splashing, but everything except Karen's voice sounded like it was coming from very far away.

"So a hungry bird gets up close to one of these caterpillars, wanting to snatch it up for dinner, and then that bird sees with its own two eyes what looks like a snake, or maybe some kind of lizard. Like the kind of beast that might want to kill it. And so that bird moves on to some other worm or insect without such a dangerous-looking face, and the caterpillar gets to live another millennium."

The last sentence she spoke had the lilt of a song to it, and he knew that it was the end of the story, but he was afraid still to turn and look at her. Afraid of what he might see in Karen's face.

He imagined—but only for a moment—how he first learned to swim. His mom would take him to the Y, and he would lie across her outstretched arms, his face in the water. She would instruct him to kick, to paddle his arms. He thought about what it might be like to wade into the pool with Karen, to hold her while she took a deep breath and then stuck her face down into the water. He thought about what it might be like to tell her to kick. To tell her that she was doing it.

When his eyes refocused on the pool, Susan Albright and his mother were cinched together in a mean embrace, like a statue, something unmovable. Their arms were strung with veins, pulsing blood the boy knew was hot, and the men were doing everything they could to keep their heads above the water and the women on their shoulders. Their chins dipped into the pool and their mouths filled with water they spit out while stumbling. But the men were still smiling on those heads attached to those straining necks. They were completely unaware, the boy thought, of how hard the women above them were going at it. Of how hard they were fighting to keep from going down.

House Calls

The sun wasn't even fully up yet and there I was, on some stranger's roof, about to begin work for the day, when this girl, maybe four or five years old, tottered down the front steps of the house across the street in an old-fashioned nurse's uniform.

There was a white cap emblazoned with a tiny red cross, a white dress with a hemline a few inches below the girl's knees, and a red shawl that hung from her shoulders like a cape. She had a stethoscope around her neck and a small nurse's bag she carried like a purse, draped over her wrist.

I imagined a grim-looking boy inside the house, her younger brother, maybe, lying on his back, pretending to be a sick old man.

The way I saw it, the two of them woke up early. She had slept in the nurse costume—something maybe her father had bought for her, even though Halloween was a good two months away—and she and her brother, crusty bits of sleep in their eyes, fell immediately into the game. The boy coughed and muttered something about his liver. The girl put her stethoscope to his chest and listened to his heartbeat. She pressed her pale fingers into his abdomen. "Does it hurt when I do this?" she asked.

"Yes," the boy said. "Right there."

The girl retrieved her nurse's bag from beside her bed and went to work. She disinfected the skin with a dry cotton ball. She opened a bandage and secured it to the boy's side, just below his ribs.

She sat vigil a little while longer, taking his pulse, placing the back of her hand against the boy's forehead to check for a fever, and then she exited the house.

In a couple of minutes, I would begin scraping the old shingles from the roof, working them loose one row at a time. I would begin carefully descending the roof's steep pitch. But an hour earlier, before Carl came to pick me up for work, I was drinking coffee and sitting in the computer room at the shelter. My shoulders and back were sore, but I managed to sit there long enough to write my wife an email. When I was finished, I wrote a separate email to my daughter and asked my wife to read it to her, please.

I'd sent similar emails the previous three mornings. I'd told my wife that I hadn't yet unpacked my bag. I'd told her I hadn't drunk a drop in days.

I won't say what I'd written to my daughter.

The girl was all the way down the front steps now and onto the sidewalk, walking away from me. She had her shoulders thrown back, her chin raised. It looked like she was headed to the next house over, to see how some other patient was doing.

She adjusted her bag, pulled it up a little on her forearm, and it took everything I had not to call out to her. Not to point to the spot on my chest and say, "Here. Come back. Let me show you where it hurts."

The First
Night Game
at Wrigley

────────────

This is the story I would tell my son about the night he was conceived.

If his mother and I had gotten married and were still together and could joyfully reminisce about this specific time and night in our lives.

If he had ever been born.

August 8, 1988

When I got back from my ten-till-two at Arby's, I didn't expect to find Kell at home, but there she was. The heat of the oven had kicked up the temperature in the already warm kitchen, and I smelled some half-recognizable herb in the air, maybe rosemary.

Without looking up at me, Kell sprinkled flour on the counter and tossed a hunk of dough on top, began smoothing it out with a rolling pin. I approached her slowly.

"Kell," I said.

She set the rolling pin down and dusted the counter with more flour.

That morning, she had straightened her hair before work, and now it was curly again, swept back under a navy blue bandana. There was a knot of dough on the shoulder of her sweatshirt, food caked on her hands and forearms. She'd been at this, I could tell, for at least a few hours.

"Bei," she said in a deep voice, mocking seriousness. Then she smiled, flashed me a sliver of the gap between her front teeth. "How was work?" Her voice was suddenly light as a pom-pom; it didn't sound like her at all.

She hunched her back and stiffened her arms, resumed smoothing out the dough. On the kitchen table there was a bowl of mixed greens tossed with cucumbers and tomatoes. A fruit salad. A tube of goat cheese and gourmet crackers. We could barely afford the rent.

I told her work was fine. I wanted to ask her the same thing, and why she was home already, but I hoped I didn't have to. I stood there in my Arby's polo holding my cap in my hand.

"I quit my job," she said. She looked up at me but kept rolling out the dough, really working it over. "In case you were wondering."

I scratched at a spot of crust on my shirt, then glanced at the oven. "You have something in there?" I asked.

"Lamb chops," she said. "We're celebrating." She quit the dough and moved to the sink, ran the hot water. "Why don't you go for some wine?"

My hand grazed the back pocket of my work slacks, where my wallet was. I figured I could charge it—the wine.

"You need anything else while I'm out?" I asked.

"Make it red," she said, and scrubbed her soapy hands under the spigot. "And none of that Australian stuff."

While I drove to the liquor store it started to rain, a summer shower. I turned on the wipers and did math in my head, trying to figure out how we were going to make the rent and take care of our student loans and credit cards. I wasn't mad at Kell, but the thought went through my head that this was not going to be good, that she may have been fucking us.

I bought three bottles of red wine from California and two tall boys of Coors Light. The guy who rang me up made small talk, like we were friends. He said something about the Cubs, and I remembered that I put on my Cubs hat before I left the house. I couldn't quite wrap my brain around what he was saying. I wondered what in the world the Cubs had to do with anything, and I wanted to ask him as much.

Instead, I said, "My girlfriend quit her job today." Just like that. Like I was letting the guy know it was raining outside. I didn't tell him that by way of this one job she'd taken editing textbooks she was making twice as much money as I was working five lunch shifts a week at Arby's and spending three nights a week on top of that loading boxes into trailers at UPS. I didn't tell him that it was only Kell's third day at the place.

"Have a good one," the clerk said.

I grabbed the paper sacks off the counter, told him I would try.

At home, the kitchen table was set, the lamb chops were cooling on top of the stove, and Kell was smoking a cigarette on the screened-in back porch. I watched her through a door off the kitchen. As if she could feel me looking at her, she asked me to pour her a glass.

The wine glasses were on the counter next to the sink, dirty, from a few nights earlier, when we celebrated her first day at the new job, so I pulled two coffee mugs out of the cabinet and filled them with wine. Kell yelled for me to bring something she could ash in, and I grabbed a third mug out of the cabinet.

What happened next was we forgot about the food for a few hours while we drank wine and watched the rain fall. This was the summer after we both graduated from college, so we were young enough to enjoy a night spent in one another's company, drinking wine and watching the rain, smelling the damp earth through the porch screen. Eventually, once the second bottle of wine was half-finished, I asked Kell about her job.

"Do we have to talk about this?" Kell asked. "You know the Cubs are on? It's the first night game at Wrigley." She dragged on a cigarette and rounded out the ash on the lip of the coffee mug. "Why don't you turn on the radio?"

I remembered the guy from the liquor store telling me something about the Cubs. I didn't want to push Kell—she obviously didn't want to talk about work—but I couldn't help myself. "I'd like to know what happened," I said.

Kell told me that she hadn't planned to leave for lunch and never go back. It was almost noon, and she had to go to the bathroom. It was the first time in her three days at this new job she'd had to go, and when she walked out of her cubicle, she realized she didn't know where the bathroom was. No one had told her. No one had told her much of anything since she'd started.

"I had to ask the janitor," she said, and took a sip of wine, "where the women's bathroom was."

I laughed a little. Kell didn't.

I wasn't sure what to say. "So the janitor," I asked, "he was able to tell you?"

I would like to think that my son would know what was going through my head right then. How I liked imagining Kell asking the janitor where the bathroom was. How I realized she could have asked anybody in the place but was most comfortable asking the guy who cleaned the toilets. I imagined the guy holding a mop in his hands and then setting the thing down in his mop bucket to walk Kell to the restroom. I imagined him smiling at her, pointing a grimy finger in the direction of the door.

And then, after I got up and turned on the radio so that we could listen to the Cubs broadcast, and I returned to the table to sit with her, I imagined Kell on those first two days at the job where no one showed her where the bathroom was. Was the third day really the first time she had to go? I imagined poor Kell's bladder about to burst a few times on the previous two days, and how she held the pee inside her so she wouldn't have to ask anybody for help. How she hoped the feeling would just go away.

———

Before I opened the third bottle of wine, I stashed the food, still untouched, in Tupperware containers and placed them in the fridge. I put away the dishes Kell had set out for us and then filled the sink with water and dishwashing liquid and settled the dirty dishes in it to soak. I wet a sponge and walked over to where Kell had rolled out the dough earlier, expecting to find the counter a mess. Instead, I found the rolled-out dough. It was stuck to the counter, and its edges had begun to harden and crack, despite the kitchen's humidity.

I was used to this kind of mess, to Kell's unfinished projects, even though I'd been living with her for only a short while. I usually found something cute and American about them, about their whimsy. But that night the disc of uncooked dough on the counter made me a little furious.

Still, I considered cleaning it up—tossing the dough in the trash and grabbing a pad of steel mesh from under the sink. I could have completed the job in just a few minutes. Instead, I decided to uncork the last bottle of wine.

I twisted the metal spiral down into the cork, and started to pull it back out, but the cork broke off. I tried to reinsert the spiral into the jagged cork but only pushed it farther down into the neck of the bottle, until it was irretrievable. I pulled a paring knife out of the drawer and stabbed the half-cork into the bottle. When I filled my mug, my hand was shaking. Bits of cork floated to the mug's surface and trembled there.

I carried the bottle onto the porch and set it as gently as I could manage on the table next to the empties. When I looked up, it had stopped raining, and Kell was outside on the patio.

"Bei," she said. "Come out here."

I stepped out onto the patio, and Kell was kneeling, running the tip of her index finger down the back of a slug. "What are you—" I asked.

Kell stopped petting the slug. "Look," she said, and made a sweeping motion with her arm, drawing my attention to the rest of the patio.

The patio was filled with slugs. Thirty, forty of them. There was a streetlight on nearby and light from the screened-in porch, and the slugs' spotted backs glistened in the wash of dim light.

"Can you believe this?" she asked.

I considered her question for a moment, watching a few more slugs crawl out of the grass onto the cement patio. Watching them glisten like the rest of them.

A few seconds later I told her to hold on. I walked inside and grabbed the saltshaker.

If I were telling this story to my son, he might not know what to make of what followed.

If I had to explain it to him, I would begin by saying that a neighbor boy had once showed me how salt sprinkled on a slug's back would kill it.

Then I would tell him that I was trying to teach his mother a lesson. That there was something about her penchant for the incomplete that I wanted to obliterate. And to do this, a few slugs were going to have to suffer.

Before I began, I asked Kell if she'd ever salted slugs before, and she didn't know what I was talking about. I thought she might be kidding. "Come on," I said. "Really? You've never done this?"

She smiled at me. I could tell she thought I was about to show her something new, something delightful. I remembered that a few minutes earlier I'd found her petting the back of a slug, and I was thrilled her expectations were all wrong.

I chose a slug that was set apart from the rest, and I knelt and sprinkled salt onto its back. Kell bent at the waist, put her hands on her knees.

The slug jerked into a little stretch. Then it started to foam, it stopped moving.

Kell let out a gasp. "It's dead?" she asked.

I told her it was.

"Give me that," Kell said, and reached for the saltshaker. I thought she was going to chide me for being cruel, that she merely wanted to take the salt away from me. But when I handed it over, Kell carried the shaker to a cluster of slugs and overturned the thing, letting four or five have it.

Once the slugs stopped moving, she looked at me, and she was so thrilled, so utterly delighted, I barely recognized her.

She moved to another cluster of slugs and tried to sprinkle the salt, but nothing came out.

She banged the saltshaker a few times against the palm of her hand, and a smattering of crystals dribbled out. "We need more," she said. She held the shaker out to me, and I took it from her.

On my way to the kitchen, I stopped on the porch to change the radio station. I was hoping for classical music. Something slow and sad with lots of strings.

Before I changed the station, Ron Santo's voice came on. The Cubs were up 3–1 going into the bottom of the fourth, but Santo said it looked like the game was going to be a wash, that it looked like they were going to have to call it a night on the first night game at Wrigley.

I turned up the volume and looked out at Kell, who was squatting now beside six or so dead slugs. The rest of the patio was covered with living slugs, still glistening dully in the light of the streetlamp, and I wondered selfishly what kind of cleanup this was going to require in the morning. I listened for a few seconds to Santo lamenting the rainout, truly heartbroken, and then I went inside for more salt.

It's hard for me to imagine what my unborn son would take from this story if he listened to it today. Would he, at the age of eighteen, find it charming that he was conceived the night his mother killed fifty-seven slugs? Would he be repulsed?

Would I mention to him what the cleanup the next morning was like? How the dead slugs, all dried up and stuck to the patio, looked like they had fallen straight out of the sky, and I scraped them from the concrete with a butter knife and then collected the mass of them inside one of the sacks our wine had come in. Or would I instead focus on the odd beauty of his mother and those slugs, withered and shimmering, on the concrete the night before?

It's possible that the boy would be most interested in the fact that his Vietnamese father, now a moderately successful lawyer, worked at Arby's and loaded trucks the summer after he graduated from college. Would I tell him how I walked to work each day ashamed of the uniform I wore? Or would I explain how those trailers at UPS seemed never to fill, how I sweated through my clothes each night and accomplished almost nothing?

He would react incredulously, no doubt, to the idea that his mother was able to commit such an act. And, if she were still around, she would look up from the half-finished sculpture she was working on, or from proofreading for the thousandth time the pages of her first novel, and she would blush and try to shrug the whole thing off like it never happened.

But the fact of it all is that she, like he, isn't around.

I have a wife and two children now, and they are wonderful. I feel wholly undeserving of them.

None of this should matter really. It's more history lesson than anything.

The Cubs played day games for seventy-four years before they ever played a night game at Wrigley. Over a million fans called the box office to get tickets to that game—everyone in America was talking about it—and then it lasted less than four full innings.

The first official night game occurred the following night, August 9, 1988. The Cubs played the Mets and won 6–4.

None of this should matter, but I have always wondered what the unfinished project that was Kell became after we decided not to have our son, and after we quit the little experiment of our post-graduation living together. I'm just not capable now of the imaginative leaps I was back then, when I could easily and happily picture her with a full bladder, going to ask the janitor where the bathroom was.

I don't know where she is, what she's doing.

I can't even imagine.

Potential

Number One Draft Pick Conflicted.

Speculation from ESPN, superimposed over leaked footage from a private batting practice four months back. The Number One Draft Pick watches from his couch, feet propped on the coffee table, the smaller version of himself in a perfect stance on TV—weight back, hands loose around the bat handle, spraying line drives all over the field. A little mechanical, he thinks, a little like a machine, but good. He has to admit, there aren't many left-handed-batting catchers—in the bigs or otherwise—with bat speed like his.

Fox Sports re-airs the clip from the draft, when he tried on the jersey and donned the cap. He is smiling in the video, a smile he practiced at home with the same intensity he used for forearm exercises, but the Number One Draft Pick can tell his heart isn't in it. The commissioner calls his name, the camera zooms in on his face, but one side of his mouth doesn't rise the way it should. Something cloudy settles behind his eyes.

He has until midnight to make his decision—sign with the club for $12M over three seasons, or go back to college for his senior year. Earn a paycheck on a team of strangers, or a degree alongside the guys he's known since he was eighteen. Begin a professional career, or risk injury another year as an amateur.

But even if he can go another college season keeping his rotator cuffs and cruciate ligaments intact, even if he can put up the same numbers that made him *Baseball America's* Player of the Year, more than one owner would probably pass on him for going back to school in the first place. No one forgets a stunt like that. The Number One Draft Pick is pretty certain you can only be the number one draft pick once.

His parents have left voicemails: they'll support him no matter what he decides.

His girlfriend said to call if he needs anything, anything at all.

His agent wants to know what the fucking holdup is. No position player in the history of the draft has signed for this kind of money. It is, he says, a win-or-get-fucked situation.

ESPN has a sound bite from last year's number one draft pick, the phenom who pitched just twelve games in the minors before his debut in The Show. The former number one draft pick says the Number One Draft Pick will sign if he wants to sign, if he believes in the team and the steps they are taking to turn things around.

The team is on its third city in fifteen years, this one in the northern Midwest, where spring seems little more than a moment and summers are spent in anticipation of football. No fanfare, a borrowed stadium, but the owners keep trying. They've been promoting the hell out of that golden-armed boy-child drafted last year, the one with the slider so sharp it makes your eyes go crossed.

Fox Sports brings on a pundit, who speculates about what signing the Number One Draft Pick might mean for the organization.

He speculates about what it might mean if they fail to sign him and waste their selection.

He speculates about what, exactly, is going through the Number One Draft Pick's head.

It's this kind of speculation that annoys the Number One Draft Pick the most. He wishes he could tell this pundit, and all of the people sitting at home like he is, flipping through sports networks and doing their own speculating—it's not about the money.

It's not about being afraid to sign to a team with the worst record in the league two years running. Losing baseball games, he thinks, is something that happens, like bad knees or calluses. A fear of losing would keep only an idiot from taking twelve million dollars.

Yet even if he could make this known, it wouldn't begin to explain what the real problem is. Because the real problem, the thing that has kept the Number One Draft Pick up at night worrying when he should be out celebrating, is a thing he can't exactly put into words. It's more of an image. A memory of a very specific moment in time.

The Number One Draft Pick is sixteen, a sophomore, and the varsity coach has just called to let him know he's traveling with the big boys tomorrow, not the jv. The Number One Draft Pick has waited for this call since late March, when he was assigned to the jv roster even though he was twice as good as the varsity catcher. He has expected it, but still he's never felt nerves like this.

The Number One Draft Pick is lying in bed, staring at the ceiling, fairly certain he won't get to sleep tonight, and what kind of varsity debut will he make tomorrow if he's nodding off behind the plate?

He gets out of bed and walks down the hall toward his parents' room. He lifts his hand to knock, but the door swings open instead. Here is his father, a balding career chemist with his round belly and shoulders only half as wide as the Number One Draft Pick's. He's wearing sagging white boxer shorts and pulling on a robe as he yawns without a sound. He slips into the hallway and pulls the door shut, then heads to the bathroom, telling the Number One Draft Pick to meet him in the kitchen.

It's not uncommon, a meeting like this. Saturday nights in the spring, when back-to-back games have left his knees aching, the Number One Draft Pick might head to the kitchen for a bag of frozen beans and find his father hunched over a legal pad, scribbling down numbers and symbols and scratching out others just as quickly. Work stuff, he says, as far as the explanation ever goes. Formulas, equations—a language as foreign to the Number One Draft Pick as the obscure hand-signals he gives his pitcher must be to his father.

He never was a baseball dad, one of those guys who shouted at the umpires or talked at your neck through the chain-link of the dugout. His father brought his own folding chair, placed it down the first-base line, and sat rubbing blades of grass between his fingers, his eyes always on something beyond the field or game in front of him.

When they meet at night they don't talk about baseball or school or his father's job at Eli Lilly. The hour excuses any conversation. His father will usually grease a baking sheet and saw off a dozen discs of frozen cookie dough, and while it bakes they will wait in a tired silence with the TV on the late-late show or a bad movie. The Number One Draft Pick has already taken the tube of dough from the freezer, but when his father arrives downstairs he digs around in the cupboards instead, coming up with a bag of chocolate chips, the double-boiler, a sack of sugar. He snags a carton of eggs from the fridge.

"I know it's late," says his father, "and I know you have a big day tomorrow. But I want to show you something." He holds up two shiny silver bowls and says it's time to get cracking. "Yolks in this one, whites in here," he says. "There should be no sunshine at all in this bowl. Make it look like the inside of a cloud."

The Number One Draft Pick has hardly ever cracked an egg, much less separated one. There are six of them, and the process grows more unnerving with each. He splits the shell and juggles the yolk between halves, certain he has never held anything so delicate in his hands, certain his thick fingers are incapable of it, that it's just not something they were meant to do. It takes time, but eventually he fills one bowl with gold and the other with murky white. The double-boiler has begun steaming on the stove, making the whole kitchen smell like chocolate, so thick and fragrant that just breathing feels like tasting. Only now does he think to ask what they're making.

"We're making a reaction," his father says, smiling now, as

animated as a TV host whisking the whites into a thick froth. "An egg yolk is all fat," he says, "but these whites are all protein. Right now I'm mixing air into them, and the protein forms a skin around the bubbles, turning it into foam."

The Number One Draft Pick can't help but laugh.

"It's a meringue," his dad confesses. "That's what it's called. We're making a soufflé. I know it sounds — you know, French — but at heart it's science. And we have to move fast now, because the air can still leak out. Hand me that bowl."

His father beats the yolks just as quickly and then combines all three colors into one — the thick gold and sudsy white and the rich brown chocolate — folding it all together until it looks and smells like the inside of a candy bar. The Number One Draft Pick has never seen his father at work, but now, watching the care he takes in greasing the baking dishes and swirling them with sugar so it coats the sides, he can imagine the man his father becomes inside a laboratory, among all the strange glassware and perfect blue flames.

"Let's fill 'em up," his father says, pouring the mixture into each of the dishes, explaining how the bubbles will expand in the oven, and the heat will stiffen the proteins, how the soufflés should explode over the top. "But still," he says, "there's no guarantee that will happen. If there was any trace of fat in the meringue, the bubbles will break. That's why I said — no sunshine. But you did fine. You did the best you could. Just like you'll do the best you can tomorrow, and whatever happens will happen."

The Number One Draft Pick lifts one of the white baking dishes, barely heavier than it had been when he held it empty. He imagines both outcomes at once: the soufflés risen, puffy like clouds, and fallen, dense as cake donuts. Why not just eat it now, he wonders. Why even risk ruining them?

And this, this is the unexplainable thing he has been thinking about ever since the commissioner called his name. That night, and how he turned on the oven's interior light and knelt at its glass window so he could watch for whatever was going to happen to them. How the whole time all he really wanted was to pull them from the oven right then and there. To keep them just the way they were.

Estate Sales

My mother-in-law, Amanda, kicked the bucket, and my father-in-law, Bill, started going to estate sales.

Bill drives a boxy red Ford truck with a handmade, wood-and-welded-iron bed extending from the cab. He spent two months of his retirement building this truck bed, and it's a sturdy, monstrous-looking thing. On the highway, he cruises steadily at forty-five miles per hour, and I often pass him in the morning when he is on his way to a sale somewhere in Illinois and I am on my way to the university where I teach. On clear, fogless mornings, I know it's his truck from about a mile back.

Bill used to be a mechanical engineer, but since his retirement, he's doing his best to look like a hillbilly—growing his hair and his beard long and brown and scraggly. When I notice his truck's handmade bed up ahead of me on the road, I sometimes get a glimpse of his brown beard blowing out the open window of his driver's side door. He looks like something from another era, but he's a whiz with email, and he carries a cell phone.

Sometimes, when I'm behind him on the road, I'll call him on his cell to find out where he's headed. He tells me the name of the town, and what the sale is featuring: a hay baler, thirteen years of *Alfred Hitchcock's Mystery Magazine*, tools. He usually sounds pretty excited, pretty with it for a widower. He'll ask me about Claire, my wife and his daughter, and about what I plan on teaching that day. For a wannabe hillbilly, he's respectful of the liberal arts. At some point, I'll pass him, beeping the cruddy horn of my Prius as I pull up alongside him. I'll show him the palm of my right hand, in a little wave, and he'll give me a two-finger deal, a kind of sideways peace sign. I'll tell him good luck at the sale, and we'll hang up.

This morning, I see the enormous bed of Bill's truck ahead of me on the road and a ribbon of his beard streaming out his open window. I whip out my phone and call him, and it rings four or five times before he picks up. "Gabriel," he says. He never calls me by my full name. It's usually "Gabe," sometimes just "G."

"William," I say back.

Bill sighs into the phone, and something inside me makes my foot tap the brake a couple times to slow down the car.

I wait for him to say something else, to ask me about Claire or what story I am going to teach that day, and when he doesn't speak, I get nervous and break the silence. "On your way to a sale?" I ask.

"No," he says. "I'm out in the woodshop, stripping an old school desk."

I can hear the wind blowing through his window, and the same NPR station I'm listening to playing behind his voice. I wonder if he can't see me yet in his rearview mirror, and I slow my Prius down even more.

I could call him on the lie, try to make a joke out of it. "Really, William," I could say. "That isn't your Ford I see half a mile ahead of me? That's somebody else's beard I see fluttering out the driver's side window?"

Bill's hairy cheeks would flush pink up there in his cab, and he would chuckle a little. "Well, actually," he would say. And then we would reconcile the thing, just like that.

Instead, I sit here listening to the wind coming through his window, to the radio. I think about how since Amanda passed, Bill's spent hours wandering through dead people's houses, looking at their paintings hanging on the walls, and their televisions and salad spinners, all of it for sale. I think about all the times he's loaded the monstrous back end of that truck with other people's stuff and how, once he gets home, he piles it all up in his garage and woodshop and living room. Lately, when Claire and I go to visit him, it's like walking through a junk shop, just trying to get to the bathroom or the refrigerator. It's something I could probably make fun of him for, or at least offer to help him get organized, but I keep quiet. Maybe someday I'll wake to find Claire not breathing in bed beside me, and things'll change.

For now, I reach up and turn the volume of my radio down all the way, and I hear Bill's voice. "Gabe?" he says. "Gabe. You there?"

I wonder how long he's been saying my name, how long I've been imagining myself inside his house.

Up ahead, I see his brake lights flash two times, and I worry I'm caught. I tap my own brakes again.

I'm doing about twenty-eight. I've never seen the highway at this speed, and it's no more majestic: row after row of corn and soybeans; a few pine windbreaks between the homesteads.

"Yeah, Bill," I say. "I'm here."

"So you on your way to school?" he asks.

"I'm just getting ready to leave the house," I say, and for a second I am back in my own house, kissing Claire on the cheek, gathering my briefcase and cup of coffee, my keys. I get a feeling inside me I've never actually had when leaving the house in the morning. Even the soybean fields look a little different, greener. "Good luck with that desk," I tell him.

"Oh, it's being a bear," he says. "Some clucks painted the thing white."

"Some clucks," I repeat, and we tell one another good-bye and hang up.

Without the radio going, I can hear the zipping sound my tires make on the road. I see Bill's brake lights flash again, and I tap mine just the same.

I set the cruise control at twenty-five, let him widen the gap between us.

Two Weeks
and
One Day

He asks her how long it is now until she takes that trip.

Two weeks, she says, *and one day*. Her feet bounce in their flip-flops. They curl and flex.

She is sitting on a brick step outside the bar. In front of her, and above the dartboards inside, there is a stained-glass window portraying abstract crows cutting through a blue sky. She holds a beer in one hand, a cigarette in the other. He stands next to her—looming and jovial and haloed by the parking lot's sodium lamps.

For the past few days, she has been asking herself, Why Tunisia?

She doesn't know thing one about the place, but the ticket has been booked for close to a month, charged to her mom's credit card. She is unrolled for next semester's classes.

Looks like you're going to have a good time, he says. *A great time.*

The stained-glass window was inspired by something created by Frank Lloyd Wright. There is a framed sheet of paper on the wall inside, next to the dartboards, explaining the connection between the window and Frank Lloyd Wright, but she has never read the note all the way through. It has something to do with one of his houses, she thinks.

The crows, even in the dark, are visible. They are never not flying.

She wonders: What language do they speak in Tunisia?

What color is the natives' skin?

Where do the people *there* fly off to when they want to get away from things, when they want to wake up one day and find themselves, just like that, in an entirely different world?

Consent

Peloma left the consent form on the dining room table with a sticky note attached to it. The form was folded into thirds as if it had been in an envelope, and the yellow note rose from the paper like a little ramp.

On the note, she had written, "Please?" and beneath that, in small block letters inside parentheses, "I can help pay." I had to squint to see it, but she'd drawn a tiny smiley face — with x's for eyes, no nose, and a smile no bigger than a comma — beneath the word "help."

Peloma played second-chair clarinet in the high school band, and earlier that month, when the German Club elected new officers, she'd been named secretary. I imagined the worst: Some fancy band camp or a trip to Munich. I figured that whichever it was, if Peloma was offering to help cover the costs, I was going to pay through the nose for it. And then on top of it all, she was going to spend quality time far away from me with people who could read sheet music or speak Deutsch.

I unfolded the form and saw that it was addressed to the parent and/or guardian of a Logansport High School sophomore. The school's use of the singular—*parent*—on forms like this used to freak me out. The first time I received a note from Peloma's grade school after Marcella died, I thought maybe it had been tailored especially to suit my widower status. Peloma was in fourth grade then, and after I got over the initial shock of the letter's greeting, I realized all they wanted was to ask if I'd allow Peloma to go on a field trip to the racetrack down in Indianapolis.

After its formal greeting, this note went on to say that the high school was no longer offering driver's education as a part of its curriculum. It would still be taught by "the qualified and certified individuals who for many years had been teaching young adults to safely and surely navigate the road," but the classes would be held at night and on the weekends, not during school hours. Because it was not a part of the school's official curriculum, the class would cost a little over three hundred dollars.

By the time I finished reading the letter, my hands were shaking. I placed the note face down on the table, and this time, when the sticky note was looking up at me, I noticed Peloma had drawn a tongue hanging out of the mouth of the tiny smiley face with *x*'s for eyes.

I shouldn't have been worried about Peloma getting her driver's license, not really, but I was. For a long time after Marcella's accident, Peloma only rode in the car with her counselor or me. Mostly just me. Her first year of high school, though, Peloma started getting involved in extracurricular activities. That's what she called them. "Extracurricular activities are important, Dad," she would say. "Colleges *love* extracurricular activities."

I would let her know that she was only a freshman and that college was still a long ways away. "Or are you looking for early admission?" I would tease. "You already have a major picked out, too?"

She would say, "Whatever, Dad," or somesuch thing, but she would smile, dismissing me in that sweet way.

At first Pell spent a lot of time at band practice, marching around the high school's parking lot in her full uniform. I drove over there on a couple Saturdays after I got off work, and it wasn't hard to pick her out from the rest. With that hat on her head, she was taller than pretty much everybody except one or two boys. But those boys didn't have hair like Peloma: long and orange and curled into spirals that were always loosening in the heat, sticking to her neck and the back of her uniform.

When I watched her walking around in formation with the clarinet in her hands, I was proud of her, of how far she'd come in the last few years, even if she was a little wobbly on those long and chubby legs.

Two years after Marcella died, Peloma had a rough time of it. She endured an early puberty that made her too tall, too big, too clumsy. And then she had to start middle school—with a dead mother and no ally in the world it seemed except me.

Because I was dealing with my own problems at the time—losing Marcella, issues at the steel factory—I didn't really understand how bad Pell had it until I found her sitting on the toilet next to a tub filled with lukewarm water after swallowing a small handful of aspirin. A few weeks later, she etched a nick into the side of her wrist with a paring knife, and then ended up staying for a short time at an institution in Indianapolis.

But together we made it through it all somehow. Meanwhile, Peloma joined the middle school band, made a couple friends, aced pretty much every test her teachers put on the desk in front of her.

And then she began high school and became interested in those extracurricular activities. There was no way I could get her to everywhere she needed to go, even if she'd let me drive her, or wanted me to. Some nights, she wouldn't come home until I was already nodding off in my chair.

It was five o'clock when I read the consent form. Peloma, I knew, probably dropped the thing off for me on a brief stop by the house before she went back out into the world. She most likely wouldn't be home for hours.

I found myself walking away from the consent form on the table and heading toward Pell's bedroom. Pell's door was closed, but all I had to do to get inside was turn the little gold-plated knob.

I hadn't been inside her room in a long time. It still looked pretty much the same as it did when she was ten. A pink curtain covering the window. A pink comforter with lots of pillows on it on the bed. A dresser. A closet with folding doors that didn't truly shut.

I walked around the end of Peloma's bed and over to her dresser. She still had Marcella's jewelry box on top of it. And now, there was a framed picture of Marcella and me next to it. The photo of us was taken at the steel factory's Christmas party. We'd gotten a babysitter for Peloma that night, and we'd dressed up. Marcella wore a cream-colored dress and high heels. I wore my good jeans and a button-down shirt with a skinny black tie knotted at my throat. We look a little tipsy in the photo, but happy. Marcella is just starting to laugh and exposing her white throat.

The mirror over Pell's dresser was a little dirty, clouded with hairspray and perfume. Around the mirror's edges, she had sticky note after sticky note with little messages written on them: "Buy greasepaint." "Call Mindy." "German Club Meeting Tuesday!" The note in the mirror's center read, "Wednesday: Study w/Crew for Bio Test at Erica's." So that's where she was right then, or where she soon would be. They would study genetics and talk about boys and eat Nutter Butters and drink Diet Mountain Dew. I would maybe shower, eat a grilled cheese sandwich, and sit down in front of the TV, hoping I could stay awake until Pell made it home.

I placed my left hand on the hardware that would allow me to open Peloma's underwear drawer. I nudged it open a little, but then stopped and looked at myself in the mirror over the dresser. I knew I shouldn't be doing this, that it was wrong, but it's not like I was snooping. I wasn't looking for drug paraphernalia or a hidden flask of liquor. All I wanted was a look at those cards she used to send to herself back when she was a somewhat suicidal middle-schooler, the ones with those half moons and stars set against a deep blue night sky. The ones that when you opened them up read "Why are you still alive?"

I pulled the drawer out all the way, and didn't see even one envelope. Which meant I was going to have to dig around a little. I maneuvered the items by pinching them between my pinky and thumb, using only the tips of my fingernails, and lifting them out of the drawer and onto the bed's pink comforter. I imagined for a bit that Marcella was watching me from the photograph on the dresser and that she had stopped smiling. After a couple minutes, the drawer was empty, and I could smell the cedar wood lining it.

The cards were gone.

I should have been happy. When I first found those cards, before I realized Peloma was sending them to herself, I thought somebody was playing a cruel trick on the girl. Torturing her. And I wanted to murder that somebody. To crush that somebody's windpipe beneath my thumbs. Then I came to understand that she was the culprit, the torturer, which made it difficult for me to breathe, as if some invisible thumb were pressing hard and quiet on my windpipe.

So I should have been happy that those days were behind us, long gone. I should have been happy that Peloma had friends, that she was right now sitting in a circle with a group of them in her socked feet talking about Gregor Mendel. But all I really wanted was a glimpse of one of those cards.

I fell asleep that night in my chair and woke up at three to a blue TV screen. I crept down the hall to see that Peloma was in bed and sound asleep beneath her comforter, and then I went to bed and set my alarm for a few hours later.

The next morning after I got dressed for work, I found Peloma cooking oatmeal in the kitchen.

"Sit down," she said. "I'll pour you some coffee."

"It's half past six. Don't you have somewhere to be?"

"Keep it up," she said, "and I'll eat all of this oatmeal myself."

Peloma had placed the morning's newspaper on the table, and I unfolded it while she poured me the coffee. "So how did it go last night?" I asked.

Peloma set the cup down on the table. "How did what go?"

I almost said something about the biology test but caught myself. "Whatever it was you were doing," I said.

She said it had gone fine, that they were probably all going to ace their biology test today. Then she scooped large mounds of oatmeal into two bowls and carried them to the table.

I set the newspaper back down and took the spoon out of the bowl of oatmeal Peloma had put in front of me. When I looked up at her sitting across from me, she had the consent form for the driver's education class in her hands.

"I assume you had a chance to look this over?" Peloma said. She set it down and took a dainty bite of oatmeal, all nonchalance.

"I did," I said. I sipped my coffee. I thought about picking up the newspaper, really ignoring her, but I kind of wanted to watch her squirm. "Strange how they're cutting it out of the curriculum, hmm?" I said. "I suppose you could say driver's ed has become an extracurricular activity."

Pell balanced her spoon on the mound of oatmeal and the rim of her bowl. "I suppose you could," she said. She wasn't quite looking at me.

"And you already participate in quite a few of those, no?"

"Yes, I do," she said. "And they're important." She picked her spoon back up and finally looked at me. "But this is different," she said. "This is how I go about getting my driver's license."

There was not much chance in the world I wasn't going to let her take the class, and I'd just been teasing her up until that point, delaying the inevitable, but Peloma seemed so desperate right then, holding her spoon over her oatmeal, her face serene, that I felt bad.

"Tell me you're going to be a great driver," I said. "Tell me you're going to be the best driver in the history of driver's ed at Logansport High School."

I thought she might backflip or cartwheel right there in the kitchen. She stood up from the table, bumping and shaking it. "Oh," she said, coming toward me. "I'm going to be an awesome driver. Spectacular."

When she got to me, I still had my arms on the table, and she gave me a vicious side-hug, her orange hair spilling across my face.

Once she finally let go of me, I said, "You better be." I started to say something else, something meaningful, but Peloma had already picked up the phone to call one of her friends. I looked back at her, and while the phone was ringing and she was waiting for somebody or other to pick up, she mouthed the words "Thank you, thank you, thank you," over and over at me.

The driver's ed classes began the first week of November. I drove Peloma to the school on a Saturday morning, and she was so excited she almost forgot to take her backpack off when she sat down in the front seat with me.

When we arrived, she scrambled to pick her backpack up off the floor like she was trying to gather money inside a wind tunnel.

"Listen," I said. "I know you do well in your classes, but this one is different."

She opened the truck's door and put one foot on the ground outside. "Don't worry," she said. "I'm going to listen harder than I ever have before in class. I'm going to take more notes. I'm going to ask more questions. I'm going to—"

"All right, then," I said. "Go."

Once she was fully out of the truck she turned, kissed the tips of her fingers, and blew the kiss in my direction. She used to like it when I would pretend to miss and then catch her blown kisses, but that morning, I kissed my own fingers and blew the kiss I'd left on them at her. I imagined our two kisses colliding right there in the cab over the console—a safe, sweet collision.

Pell closed the door and swung her backpack over her shoulders and set off up the walk that led to the school's doors, joining a small crew of fellow sophomores who were paying to take a class at a public school, who would soon be driving the streets of Logansport with the rest of us.

I stayed parked next to the curb for a minute or two and watched a few more kids enter the school. I kind of wished that the driver's ed classes were going to be held outside, like marching band practice, so I could hide somewhere and watch her. I would have liked to watch Pell raise her hand to ask a question about something she didn't understand, like how to read the lines on a two-lane highway and know whether it was okay to pass some Sunday driver lollygagging along in front of you. I would have liked to watch her jot down the teacher's answer in her notebook. Maybe she would draw a little diagram. Maybe she would make a note to herself to ask me for some further clarification later.

For two weeks, I drove Pell to classes on Wednesday nights and Saturday mornings. She listened to lectures and took tests, and sometimes she'd bring home as many as three exams she'd aced during one long session. She hung these tests on the refrigerator, where Marcella used to hang Pell's art projects and spelling tests when she was just a kid.

On the third Saturday of classes, after I spent the day by myself raking and bagging leaves, I picked Pell up at school, and she announced that they were going to begin their behind-the-wheel training the next day, on Sunday afternoon. She had to be at the school at one, at which time she and two of her classmates would get inside a car with Mr. Burroway.

"You mean they let the same guy who teaches Shakespeare teach you how to drive?" I asked. "Couldn't you have gotten the shop teacher? Maybe a janitor or lunch lady?"

Pell's backpack was balanced on her knees. She buckled her seatbelt. "You think because he knows most of *Hamlet* by heart he doesn't know how to properly use a turn signal or merge into traffic?"

I started the truck. "I guess I'd be more comfortable if you were going to learn from somebody who didn't pay to have his oil changed."

"Whatever you say, Clem. Mr. Burroway's only been teaching driver's ed for about the past twenty years." She set her backpack in the floor of the cab.

"I'm sure he'll be great," I said. "And you can still call me 'Dad,' you know."

"Yeah," she said. "I know." Laughing a little, she leaned forward to adjust the channel and volume on the radio.

I was only joking about Mr. Burroway, who had actually taught me senior English a long time ago, when he was younger and hadn't yet started to earn extra money on the side teaching driver's ed. He was a short and serious man, just the kind of guy that was needed, I thought, to maintain the peace as he let three fifteen-year-olds take their first trips around town behind the wheel.

The next morning, Pell was sitting on the couch in the living room by eight o'clock, pretending to drive. She held her shoulders back, and kept her chin raised, as if posture were somehow paramount. Her hands were at ten and two, and she seemed to squeeze the invisible steering wheel in front of her with an odd combination of strength and delicacy.

"Left turn," she announced, and then she moved her left hand to where the turn signal would be and pushed it down. She retuned her hand to the wheel, tapped the brakes with her right foot, and began turning the invisible wheel using a hand-over-hand motion.

"Nicely done, Andretti," I said. "What are the conditions like on the track this morning?"

"The conditions are solid," she said. "This girl is ready to drive."

"How about we go out for some breakfast?" I said. "Girl needs her energy, no?"

"It won't be long and I'll be driving you to breakfast on Sunday mornings," she said, and I told her that was true, and to go and get ready.

A few hours later, I dropped her off at the school, and the cars with those orange wedges on top that read "Student Driver" were parked near the side entrance.

"There they are," I said. "Your wheels."

Peloma was so excited she couldn't speak. She just stared at the line of parked cars with her mouth hanging slightly open.

I told her to have a good time, and to be careful, and she reminded me of what she'd already learned in class—that the cars have brakes on the passenger side so the instructor can stop the car anytime he wants to.

"All right, then," I said. "Go. I'll see you in a few hours."

I could have stuck around that afternoon. I could have found a place to hide and watch Peloma as she walked out of the school with her driving group and Mr. Burroway and found the Chevy that they'd all be driving around the parking lot and the road that circled the school. Maybe they'd turn into one of the nearby residential neighborhoods and get some practice at four-way stops.

I could have stuck around and watched all that, proud and full of wonder, but I didn't. And so when I picked Peloma up a few hours later, I didn't know what to expect, the way I could have.

I had thought maybe we'd go for ice cream or cheeseburgers to celebrate her first day driving, but as soon as Pell got in the car she started crying so hard her whole body shook.

"What is it?" I said. "What's wrong?" I could tell she'd been holding this back for a while, waiting for me to come pick her up. She was barely breathing.

"Just drive," she said, so I started the truck and drove away from the school.

It was only six o'clock, but dusk was already setting in. I drove through the residential neighborhoods around the school, where the tops of leafless trees glowed orange, backlit by the setting sun. It seemed as good a time and place as any to cry, and so I stayed quiet and listened to Peloma as her breathing began to steady. She wiped the tears away from her eyes with the backs of her hands a couple minutes later, and once I pulled out onto Main, she had regained all of her composure. She began to tell me what had happened.

When her group was walking outside with Mr. Burroway, Pell had volunteered to take the wheel first. Mr. Burroway handed her the keys and muttered a brief line from some Shakespeare play. Pell was too excited to catch it, and in a few seconds she had fastened her seatbelt and was behind the wheel with the keys in her hand.

Which is when she realized she hadn't ever actually started a car before.

She calmed herself with deep breaths and sank the key into the ignition. Her two fellow drivers were in the back, seatbelt straps across their chests. Mr. Burroway placed a hand on the console between Pell and him, and told her she could start the car whenever she was ready.

She turned the key, she said, and the engine came to life. When she placed her hands on the steering wheel, she could feel it, for some reason, in her teeth.

She managed to lift her foot off the floor of the car even though it felt like her shoe was full of wet sand, and place it on the brake. She managed to put the car into reverse. With her foot still on the brake, it occurred to her in this way that filled her with complete surprise that once she moved her foot to the gas pedal, the car was going to move, and that she would be in control of it.

She didn't know how long she sat there with her foot on the brake, but it was long enough that Mr. Burroway asked her if she was okay. He encouraged her to reverse the car out of the parking spot, to go ahead and move her foot from the brake to the gas pedal.

Pell's eyes closed just before she finally lifted her foot onto the gas pedal. Then she opened them and looked into the rearview mirror, and then at her hands on the steering wheel. She was going to do this.

And then she punched the gas so hard that her head snapped back against the headrest. Mr. Burroway's foot immediately hit the brake on his side of the car, and Pell's head whiplashed again. The kids in the backseat cursed and then laughed, covering their mouths with their fingers.

The car was about a third of the way out of the parking space, and Pell's hands felt slippery on the steering wheel. Mr. Burroway said, "You don't need to push quite so hard on the pedal."

Pell couldn't catch her breath. It was like she was trying to breathe for three or four people at once. Her hands were still attached to the steering wheel, and when she tried to move them, she couldn't. Eventually, she asked Mr. Burroway if someone else could drive. He consented without seeming to give it much thought, and so she turned the ignition off, unfastened her seatbelt, and exited the car and switched places with the girl who'd been sitting behind her. Once Pell was in the backseat, it took everything she had to keep from crying.

Pell moved her hands in the air as she told me all of this. She was animated, herself again. By the end of the story, the sun had almost fully set, and we were sitting in my truck in our driveway.

Listening to Pell tell it all, I couldn't help but feel guilty. Shouldn't I have taken her out at some point and let her start the truck and feel the engine come to life beneath her? Shouldn't I have shown her the proper way to accelerate and reverse?

By the time we were in the driveway I had made up my mind about something, though I hardly knew it. I began to put the truck into park, to tell Peloma that she'd do better next time, that she'd do fine, but instead I put the truck into reverse, looked over my shoulder, and backed out of the driveway.

"Where are you going?" Pell said. "What's going on?"

"We're going back up to the school," I said.

"Dad," Pell said. "You don't have to talk to my teacher. I can handle this."

I told her that I wasn't planning on talking to her teacher. "I'm putting you back behind the wheel," I said.

Pell's hand reached out toward the glove compartment. She touched it with only the tips of her fingers. Then she reached down to her backpack and withdrew a pen from one of its pockets. She uncapped the pen, and out of the corner of my eye, I watched her draw a circle in black ink on the inside of her pale and puffy wrist.

"Can't we do it some other time?" she said. "Do we have to do it now?"

The sky wasn't full dark yet, but the streetlights were on, casting pale light. I noticed for what was probably the first time that fall that there were no bugs in the air.

I told Pell that now was as good a time as any. I told her there was nothing to be afraid of, that plenty of people, even stupid people, had been learning how to drive cars for years.

"Yeah," she said, "but . . ." She drew x's for eyes inside the circle on her wrist, then added a flat little line for a mouth.

It would have been easy enough for her to complete what she'd started to say — Yeah, but not all of those people had mothers who died in car crashes — but I didn't want to hear her say it.

"You'll be a great driver," I said. "You'll be fine."

When we reached the school, I turned onto the road that ringed it, and followed it until I reached one of the parking lots reserved for teachers. Behind the shop classes, between the school and a small woods. The lot was shaped like a perfect rectangle, and I parked the truck in the middle of it, left the engine running, and got out.

When I got to Pell's door, she still hadn't opened it up. She had the palms of her hands on her thighs. Through the window, I could see half of that unsmiling face on the inside of her wrist, and one of its eyes, a tiny x.

I opened the door. "Come on," I said. "Get moving, girl."

I settled into the passenger seat while Pell walked around the truck, squatted gingerly into the cab, and closed the door. The parking lot was truly dark. There were a few lampposts, and the truck's headlights cast bright beams in front of us, but it felt like we could have been anywhere, just the two of us in the truck's cab, preparing to move through the darkness.

I had her turn off and restart the ignition a couple times, so she could get used to it. Then I had her idle while the truck was in drive and reverse, so she could see how the truck moved even when you didn't give it any gas.

I had Pell drive forward and pull into a parking space and then back out of it. When she hit the gas the first few times, she sent both of our heads rocking back toward our headrests, but she got the hang of it. I had her drive from one end of the parking lot to the other, and then I told her to put it in reverse and take us all the way back to where we'd started. She turned in the seat and left one hand on the wheel while she backed up, looking out the back window. I focused on the headlights' beams, watched as where we'd been drew farther and farther away from us.

Once Pell backed up all the way to the edge of the parking lot, she put the truck into park and looked at me. There was a hint of smile on her face. She was glad we'd done this, I could tell. "Is that good?" she asked. "Can we go get something to eat now?"

"Not yet," I said. I was enjoying sitting in the passenger seat. I could see us doing this kind of thing a couple nights a week until Pell finished driver's ed. She would want the practice, and I would want to sit there beside her just like I was.

"You know the rules of the road," I said. "You've passed all those tests. Now drive us home."

Pell didn't even hesitate. She pulled out of the parking lot, drove the road that circled the school, and eventually we were headed home. She made double-stops at all of the stop signs and slowed down more than she needed to at green lights, just in case they were about to change, but in a few minutes we were almost there.

Neither one of us spoke while she drove. The radio wasn't on.

I could tell she was aware of me there beside her, but once she turned onto the road where we lived, it wasn't hard to imagine her doing all this without me. It wasn't hard to imagine her on some two-lane highway, or the interstate even. One foot on the gas pedal, the other tapping to some song playing on the radio. Her hand thrust out the open window, its palm flat, moving up and then down in the rush of wind as if she were signaling to turn, or running her hand over the back of a series of small waves that kept crashing and crashing. That seemed never to stop.